Sherri L. King

Lover's ey

Ellora's Cave
Romantica Publishing

Edwardsville Public Library
112 South Kansas Street
Edwardsville, IL 62025

An Ellora's Cave Romantica Publication

www.ellorascave.com

Lover's Key

ISBN 9781419961649
ALL RIGHTS RESERVED.
Lover's Key Copyright © 2009 Sherri L. King
Edited by Kelli Collins.
Cover art by Darrell King.

This book printed in the U.S.A. by Jasmine-Jade Enterprises, LLC.

Electronic book publication October 2009
Trade paperback publication September 2010

The terms Romantica® and Quickies® are registered trademarks of Ellora's Cave Publishing.

With the exception of quotes used in reviews, this book may not be reproduced or used in whole or in part by any means existing without written permission from the publisher, Ellora's Cave Publishing, Inc.® 1056 Home Avenue, Akron OH 44310-3502.

Warning: The unauthorized reproduction or distribution of this copyrighted work is illegal. Criminal copyright infringement, including infringement without monetary gain, is investigated by the FBI and is punishable by up to 5 years in federal prison and a fine of $250,000.
(http://www.fbi.gov/ipr/)

This book is a work of fiction and any resemblance to persons, living or dead, or places, events or locales is purely coincidental. The characters are productions of the author's imagination and used fictitiously.

LOVER'S KEY
സ

Trademarks Acknowledgement
☙

The author acknowledges the trademarked status and trademark owners of the following wordmarks mentioned in this work of fiction:

Hayabusa: Suzuki Motor Corporation

Invader Zim: Viacom International Inc.

Nag Champa: Shrinivas Sugandhalaya

Publishers Clearing House: Publishers Clearing House LLC Ltd. Liab. Co.

Smithsonian National Museum of Natural History: Smithsonian Institution Trust Instrumentality

SpongeBob SquarePants: Viacom International Inc.

Twinkie: Continental Baking Company

Prologue

"Come on you rat bastard, I know you're in there somewhere, *somehow*," Brandi Carroll sobbed under her breath as she tightened her fists around the baseball bat. "Let's not take all night."

She shifted her weight on the foot of the toddler's bed and held her eyes glued to the closet door closed directly in front of her. It was well past midnight, the hour she had hoped to resolve this situation. But one couldn't count on monsters to be punctual all the time. She held back a yawn and twisted her neck until she heard and felt a satisfying pop in her joints. It had been a very long night, and it looked as if it wouldn't be ending for a while yet.

Brandi looked away for a moment, resting her burning eyes. She saw the moon peeking out from behind some stray clouds through the window, and the room was suddenly alive with light. Shadows stretched and became looming bogeymen, monsters all, and they crept with alien movements ever closer to the foot of the bed. But the closet door remained closed and Brandi knew this meant the real monster still had yet to arrive.

An odd sound in the stillness alerted her and she flashed her eyes back to the closet, alert at once.

Nothing.

But Brandi knew that sound, that tiny explosion of noise, which had nothing to do with the normal groaning and settling of the house. She could feel it down in her bones—the monster had surely come. The sound came again, this time louder, and Brandi raised the bat up high over her head in stoic trepidation, rising soundlessly from the bed and gingerly stepping closer to the closet despite the desperate pounding of her heart, which begged her instead to turn and flee.

The shadows grew and a chill breeze stirred in the room, despite the closed and locked window. Brandi felt it toy with her hair and caress her cheek. It made her shudder uncontrollably. The time would soon be at hand, she was almost certain. She had to steady herself, calm her frayed nerves, or she knew she would never be able to face this thing.

She determinedly straightened to her full height and then braced her legs wide apart like a linebacker prepared to defend his title.

The knob of the closet door turned slightly. Brandi had to blink twice, hard, just to be sure she hadn't imagined the small movement. The sound of the turning knob echoed through her mind, and Brandi knew this time she would at last get to see the monster—all of him. And perhaps, if fate were kind, she could kill it before it managed to kill her.

But first, she wanted to see the ghost, the monster, the demon, whatever it was. She wanted to look in its face, if it even had one, and know that she was the one to finally kill the vile creature once and for all. She wanted to see the nightmare through with her own eyes wide open.

The knob turned fully and the closet door cracked open with a sigh. Brandi waited, hardly knowing what to expect. She had never actually seen the monster up close and personal—only its nebulous shadow as it retreated into the closet with her nephew in tow just the night before. Would it be a gruesome sight, one that perhaps would scar her forever just by looking at it? Would it come for her or would it turn away the moment it knew an adult, and not a child, resided within the room, waiting? Could she catch it—hurt it, *kill* it— in time, before it fled back to whatever world had spawned it? She meant to try with all her might. But would that be enough?

Brandi pushed all doubts from her mind and focused with searing intensity on the crack in the door as it grew steadily wider.

Chapter One
Three years later…

ಬಿ

Brandi ignored the curious stares as she went about getting her groceries. She had long grown used to the stares, fortunately, though it had taken her quite a while. She knew the people in her small town of Mt. Airy all thought she was a little bit crazy. Hell, some of them thought she was a complete lunatic. But she didn't mind. She was a woman on a mission, and throughout history such women had often been ostracized for one reason or another. Why should she be any different in this so-called modern age?

Whispers reached her ears, buzzing around her like a swarm of flies. She couldn't quite make out the words, so she ignored this rudeness as well, for it came with the territory of being the town freak. And besides, she already pretty much knew what they were saying without having to hear it verbalized.

"She actually believes in ghosts, that girl."

"Stays up all hours of the night, hunting for the monster she says stole her nephew, though I think she may be the one who got rid of the poor boy."

"All those lost children, do you think she had anything to do with those, too?"

"When she's not in those poor parents' homes, she stays every night there in that old house, all alone. There's no telling what she does up there all night, but I'm sure it isn't sleeping."

Brandi had heard it all. From accusations of murder to pitying glances from those who thought her mad, none of it surprised her anymore. And again, she didn't care. She knew things that none of the people could understand, and she understood that her life was simply an enigma to them because of it. It was something she had to live with each and every day of her life.

She took her purchases up to the crowded checkout line, which parted before her like the Red Sea before Moses. All eyes turned to stare, but she didn't let it bother her. The cashier, a young teenager Brandi did not recognize, seemed more than eager to get Brandi through the line and out of her store, and quickly rang her up with no attempt at pleasant conversation. Brandi supposed there were a couple of decent things about being the local pariah.

The crowd watched her leave, and Brandi could have sworn she heard a collective sigh of relief. She loaded up her old pickup truck with her purchases, ignoring the dozens of missing children signs posted everywhere as best she could, and began the long drive back to her sister's house.

Her half sister, Gail, didn't live there anymore. She simply couldn't bear the house after the loss of her youngest son. But Gail kept the payments up and let Brandi live there after she had lost her job as a third-grade teacher. It was a kindness that Brandi truly appreciated.

After all, schools made it a point not to keep "crazy" people on their staff.

Brandi had hated and mourned the loss of her job. She'd greatly enjoyed being a teacher, the daily challenges, the looks on her students' faces when they had a flash of understanding on any given subject, and so much more. But unfortunately, all that was past her now. These days she simply took odd jobs from her more kindhearted neighbors to get by and ate a lot of grits, cornbread and ramen noodles to save on her food budget. There had been no time to look for a new job, even if she'd wanted to, which she didn't. Brandi kept herself very busy these days with other, more pressing matters.

The warm summer sun beat down on her arm as she stuck it out the window, letting the wind caress her fingers. The air in the truck was hot and stifling, but the breeze through the open windows toyed playfully with her hair, drying the sweat that beaded her brow. She made her last turn down a long, winding dirt road that would lead her to her half sister's big Tudor-style house nestled deep in the woods, and gave a huge sigh of relief that her bi-weekly trip into town was finally over.

She grabbed her bags and entered the house, closing the door firmly behind her. Sunlight streamed through the naked windows, banishing all the shadows within the house. The central air was on, a gentle breeze from the vents that kept the house at a cool seventy-two degrees, dispersing the heat from the sun that blazed through the windows. Brandi took her bags to the kitchen, passing by two closets, which had been boarded up. Rough planks of wood haphazardly nailed to the frames of the doors made them virtually inaccessible.

Brandi wanted them to stay that way.

After putting away her meager groceries, she grabbed an old magazine—one she'd already read many times—and kicked back in her favorite well-worn recliner with a glass of ice cold sweet tea. The magazine was a diversion from her constantly troubled thoughts, a gossip mag that would help her forget her worries for a short while. Blessedly, before she knew it, an hour had passed and the sun was sinking low over the horizon.

The phone rang, making her jump.

She answered on the third ring. "Hello?"

"Brandi," said the somewhat familiar voice on the other end.

"Mrs. Marche." She swallowed hard, palms growing damp. "I've kind of been expecting you to call." The admission stung her lips.

"My son Tyler has been missing for four days." The woman's voice was choked by tears. "But you knew that. If I let you come in here can you tell me how to find him?"

Brandi closed her eyes and prayed for strength. "I don't find children, Mrs. Marche. I wish I could, but I haven't found any of them."

"But you can tell me if someone, some person, took him or…" She faltered.

There was no use pretending she didn't know what the distraught woman really meant. "I'm not sure the monster will show itself after two days. I usually only get results the first night after the abduction."

"Please, I don't know where else to turn."

"Well, there aren't any set rules that I know of. It's possible, if I tried, I might find something to show you. But are you sure you want to go down this road?" Brandi asked warningly.

The sound of Mrs. Marche's weeping hurt Brandi's heart to hear. "I'll do anything you tell me to. The police aren't doing anything to find my baby, or the other children that have gone missing in the past several months. I heard that you helped the Ingrams before they moved away. Can you help me too?"

Brandi licked her dry lips. "I didn't help the Ingrams. I just showed them what I see. I showed them what took their child."

"I just want to know if there's any hope left for my baby," Mrs. Marche sobbed.

It was a testament to how desperate the Marches had grown in the four days since their son went missing that Brandi was even having this conversation. The Marches had once been among the throng of townspeople who seriously questioned Brandi's sanity.

"Did little Emiline sleep in the same room as Tyler?" Brandi asked after a long, weighty silence.

"Yes she does," Mrs. Marche replied. "But my daughter didn't see anything the night Tyler—"

"Has she been having bad dreams?" Brandi interrupted. "Night terrors? Anything like that since it happened?"

"Y-yes," Mrs. Marche said on a shuddering sigh. "But the doctors say it's not unusual."

"Anything else?" Brandi pressed, biting back her impatience—doctors weren't going to help Emiline.

The woman's words came in a rush, as if she were embarrassed to even utter them. "She's scared of the dark. She was never afraid of it before. If we don't turn the lights on as soon as the sun starts to set, she screams until we do." There was another sob. "We've let her sleep with us in our room for the past two nights and that seems to have helped. W-why do you ask?"

Brandi closed her eyes. "You know why I'm asking."

Mrs. Marche chuckled but the sound held no mirth. "I can't believe I'm having this conversation."

Brandi's lips twisted wryly. "I understand. Half the time even I think this is all ludicrous." She took a deep breath. "Well, I can come to your house but I can't promise you anything. Whether a human took him or something else, I can't give you any peace of mind. I'm sorry."

"I just want to know what happened to my son." Mrs. Marche's voice was emphatic. "If he was taken by this thing you say you've seen, I want to know. I'll believe you, whatever you say. I want to know if there's any hope left for us."

"There's always hope." Brandi said the words but she didn't really believe them. Not after all that she had witnessed. Not anymore.

"I'm scared to death that Emiline might be next. The Appletons lost both their children."

"I know. I'm sorry for that."

"They wouldn't listen to you. I didn't either. I'm sorry."

Rubbing her temples, Brandi saw in her mind's eye the screaming, weeping mother of the Appleton children. "They wouldn't listen to me when I told them to destroy the closet after Bebe's disappearance. If they'd listened they might have saved Suzette. Then again, maybe not."

Mrs. Marche let out a shuddering breath. "Do you really think it would have helped?"

"I know it would have been better than doing nothing. And what's more is they know it too. I showed them the monster that preyed on their children, they saw it, but they couldn't believe what they saw. The very next day they had what they thought was a rational explanation for it, something about drinking too much wine. They saw the monster and still they let Suzette sleep in that room, without tearing down the closet like I warned them to. They were afraid to believe any of it."

"I want to save Emiline. And I want to know what happened to my son."

"I can be there in twenty minutes. You'll have to let me spend the night in the kids' room. You have to prepare yourself for the unexpected. And you have to promise me that if I see what I expect to see, you will immediately tear down the closet in their bedroom. It hurts me as much as anyone when a child is lost because I couldn't do something about it. I won't waste my time or my tears if you aren't willing to act."

"I promise," Mrs. Marche said passionately. "Just please, help me. Help my family."

"I don't know if I can," Brandi warned softly.

"Try. Please."

"I'll be there in twenty minutes," Brandi said and hung up the phone. She sighed and rested her head in her hands.

"Here we go again," she said to the empty, shadowy house. There was no reply, and for that Brandi was infinitely glad.

* * * * *

Brandi sat gingerly on the foot of the racecar toddler bed, which faced the closed closet door, and waited. In one hand she held her high-powered flashlight, in the other a small video camera equipped with night vision. She had long ago given up her baseball bat—it didn't work on the monster anyway. Only light could dispel the creature. But before she flashed her light on its form, she wanted to get enough video to convince the Marches that they needed to protect their remaining child.

There was no doubt in Brandi's mind that it was the monster behind this disappearance. Just as it was responsible for the several other disappearances in town. She was certain there was no serial kidnapper on the loose as the police in the area had claimed. She could feel it, deep in her bones, and Brandi had grown accustomed to believing in her strange sixth sense. It hadn't steered her wrong yet.

The dark in the children's room was cloying and malevolent. Despite her vast experience with these situations, Brandi still felt her heart race painfully in her chest. Would the monster show itself tonight, she wondered? Or had it grown wise to her presence and decided to move on to the next family in town? She fervently hoped not. She didn't think the town could survive one more child's disappearance.

But she had no way of ensuring that didn't happen. She had no idea how to destroy the creature, only how to disperse it. She'd searched and searched for a way to get rid of it for good. She had researched endlessly at the local library and on her home computer, but to no good end. Only myths and legends could be found concerning the boogeyman of children's stories, nothing solid and real. It seemed that no one else in the world had encountered a problem like the one brewing in Mt. Airy, Georgia.

The grandfather clock in the foyer struck midnight.

"All right you asshole," Brandi growled softly. "I'm ready for you."

Lover's Key

The knob on the closet door turned infinitesimally. Brandi would have completely missed the movement if she hadn't been so focused on the closet.

She stood up and raised the camera before her, simultaneously hitting the record button with her thumb. The doorknob rattled, a loud explosion of sound in the darkness, and Brandi braced herself for what she knew would happen next.

The closet door flew open, slamming back against the wall with deafening force. The room grew cold, so cold that Brandi could see her breath in the air, and she had to fight the urge to shiver. She kept her hands steady through sheer force of will, and carefully aimed the camera at the shadow that began growing from within the darkness of the closet.

All the shadows grew long within the room, gathering and spreading. But these shadows were not nearly half as dark as the one coming toward her. Inky black, with no trace of light from within or without, the darkness grew and grew until it towered over her like an evil specter from a fairytale.

Brandi had to bite her lip until it bled, just to keep her courage from waning. She tried and failed to keep the cold sweat from beading at her temples. She began to shudder uncontrollably. She had enough wits to note there seemed to be no sound in the room now, not the chirping of the crickets outside nor the expected settling of the old house. All was silent as the grave.

The blackness took a form, that of an enormously tall humanoid. But there was no face. There were no features to mark it as anything other than a faceless monster. It reached out a nebulous hand, its arm several feet long, grasping for her. Brandi sucked in a huge breath of air and nearly choked on it, but held the camera steady despite her growing terror.

The hand passed mere inches before her face, she felt the icy cold blast of it, and she could hold back her fear no more. She turned the flashlight on, closing her eyes against the sudden glare. She heard the scream—the sound of a thousand lost souls crying out for help—and cried out herself despite her valiant effort to hold the sound back.

The scream grew louder and Brandi heard the faint noises of the Marches banging on the bedroom door, which would not open, Brandi knew, until the monster had left. The flashlight illuminated the room, breaking apart the shadows. The dark form before her shrank back, retreating once more to the closet.

"Don't you dare come back here again, motherfucker," she screamed out, losing all composure. "Go back to where you came from and leave these poor kids alone!"

The sound of the monster's scream threatened to shatter the windows. The shadow fled, turning its back on her. It shrank into the closet, rolled in on itself, and disappeared.

The closet door slammed closed just as the bedroom door flew open. The Marches, clad only in their pajamas and stocking feet, spilled into the room.

"What was that?" Mrs. Marche asked in a small, frightened and quivering voice.

Brandi realized she'd been holding her breath and let it out with an audible whoosh. "That, my friends, was the boogeyman," she said and promptly, inelegantly, passed out at their feet.

Chapter Two

The relentless, savage heat of the Arabian Desert cooled as the indigo darkness of night stealthily approached. The world lie quiet, the cooling sands still, and not a single animal or insect stirred to break the sacred twilight silence. The desert held its breath in anticipation of the setting of the punishing sun, both tentative and eager to greet the birth of silvery moonlight.

As the first ebon shadows spread across the glittering quartz, the scorching temperature dived and a blessedly cool breeze stirred the air, setting the grains upon the ground to waltz frantically until a low hum of singing sand filled the world with music. The land stirred, the ground thrumming beneath shifting dunes to reveal slumbering serpents and day-drunk insects, called to their nocturnal chores by the twinkling stars now glittering in their blanket of crystal netting around the dome of the sky. The wind called forth the feral cats from their burrows and their prey, the desert mice, shivered. There was song and there was blood and all was set in motion by the whim of the setting sun.

Solitary and jutting, a mighty stone edifice towered over the shifting sands, launching its somber grey shadow upon the moonlit dunes. It was the castle of a great landowner, or oil baron, or some other such person of import and wealth, but the desert and its children paid no respect. The wind swept the silica grains into every crack and seam of the walls, impervious to the owner's belief that this fortress was impenetrable. Not even the mountains could withstand the march of sand and survive unconquered, not even Methuselah had outlasted the Earth.

These men with guns that crawled like termites within the guard towers were oblivious to the inevitability of their downfall, for in their minds the desert was a slow adversary, one that could be held back for the immediate present with naught but a broom. But the sea of sand knew different and abided with the surety of its knowledge.

Murmurs of conversation from within the walls harmonized with the song of the shifting dunes. Men and women grunted sighs of passion, moans of lust, the symphony of lovers and eventide. Children quarreled, laughed and played. Guards tended their guns until the scent of gun oil commingled with the fragrance of cooking spices wafting from open windows. The night trembled with sound and the air hung heavy with perfume.

It was a night like any other. Save that it was a new night, one full of mystery and magic. Full of approaching hours that held promise and surprise, for each hour was a stranger and its introduction could bring unimagined wonders. Unanticipated horrors.

The breeze stilled. The sounds of living fell with it, needing the wind to be carried out into the world beyond the castle walls. The serpents stilled their slithering. The cats and mice held truce. The dunes ceased their singing. And armed men felt the hackles rise on the napes of their necks. Men, women and children all looked out into the desert, breath held, instincts warring.

The silence deepened.

Desert exploded, a mushroom cloud of sand surging outward toward the fortress gates. An immense wall of Earth and wind heaved with unforgivable force against the edifice, made pathetic and weak in the path of war.

Three shadowed figures materialized within the heart of the maelstrom, rising from the desert womb as if born from it, their presence oozing menace and purpose with each stride that marched them closer to the keep.

A man with midnight black hair and fair skin approached the nearest wall. He placed his hand on the still-warm stones, then, without aid of a rope or pick, he began to scale it like an experienced mountain climber. He shot up the steep vertical surface, moving with such alien motion that he resembled a reptile or an insect as he effortlessly ascended.

The guards came out of their initial shock as if waking from a dream. Loud explosions of gunfire filled the air, breaking the evening stillness. A man with bright blond hair and darkly bronzed skin now approached the gate, ignoring the violence around him, unafraid and uncaring of the bullets that whizzed by. He kicked at the great wooden doors only once and the wood splintered with a loud explosion of sound. The heavy doors gaped wide before him, barely hanging on by their hinges, slamming back against the walls behind them.

The third man, a very tall and imposing figure with long, dark brown hair held fastened at his nape in a leather tie, followed the blond man through the broken doors. His movements were casual and easy, though the brightly burning inquisitiveness of the icy blue eyes set deep into his tanned face was anything but. He took in the scene before him, missing nothing, and lifted his gun at the ready. He fired it in rapid succession, felling three of their foes at once and causing a cry of alarm to fill the air within the imposing fortress walls.

The man with black hair reached the top of the wall he had climbed and snapped the neck of the nearest guard before the man could even squeeze off a shot from his automatic weapon. The dark man moved so fast that his motions were a blur to the human eye, making it impossible for the guards to follow his movements. He used this magic to his advantage, effortlessly felling two more guards in mere seconds, never once allowing his foes to fire off a single shot.

A guard rushed at the blond-haired man, screaming invectives in Farsi, knife held at the ready. He stabbed the man in the heart, letting out a great cry of triumph as he did so. The hilt of the knife trembled as the blond drew in a deep, shaky breath.

Thick black smoke wafted up around the wound. The blond grabbed the hilt of the knife and pulled it from his body with a wince, sending more black smoke pouring from the wound. He tossed the knife to the ground and pulled open the hole in his fatigues where the weapon had entered his body. The torn skin fused together almost immediately, the wound healing completely within a few short seconds.

Screaming in his native Farsi, naming the blond a devil, the Arabic man fled in a panic.

The blond bent down, retrieved the knife that had wounded him and swiftly threw it at the man's retreating back. The weapon imbedded itself in the man's spine, killing him instantly, and he fell to the ground in a heap.

"Quit playing around, Marduk," the brown-haired man admonished, "and look for the spear."

Marduk gave a cocky smile to his comrade. "Yes sir, my lord Julian." He turned and made his way deeper into the throng of panicked people, ignoring their chaos as he went.

Julian turned and spotted the black-haired man as he revealed his long incisors and bit into the neck of a captive. "Ramiel, you can feed later. We need to find the spear."

Ramiel dropped his prey at his feet and licked his lips clean of blood. "I was just getting to that," he growled in a deep, commanding voice.

Julian turned and fired his gun at an approaching guard. He made his way deeper into the complex, ignoring the few women who lingered out of sheer panic, focusing only on the men who dared to attack him. His gun spat fire over and over again, and he easily felled all those who got in his way.

The wind picked up, throwing sand throughout the air in the deepening night. Sight became limited and the guards stumbled clumsily through the din. Ramiel used the advantage well, slipping through the sandstorm with ease, swiftly felling many foes along the way.

Julian went deep into the castle, ignoring the sandstorm, and almost immediately saw what he had come for. "They didn't hide it very well," he murmured to himself. "Perhaps they didn't know the value of this treasure." He approached a nook in the stone wall. Illuminated and locked, a small glass safe nestled within the nook held that which they had been seeking.

"The spear of destiny," Ramiel breathed.

"Here, let me." Marduk stepped up beside Julian and shoved his fist into the glass of the case, breaking it with little effort.

Julian reverently took the spear from its resting place. Though it was more like the tip of a spear, it was so short. It could have been no longer than twelve inches in length. It seemed that the long wooden handle had long since rotted away, leaving only the weighty bronze of the spear tip behind. Julian gently slipped it into the folds of his fatigues for safekeeping. "We now have five of the seven keys. Let's get the hell out of here," he said to his two friends, stepping away from the wall.

A dozen armed men turned a corner and began to charge them, screaming their war cries into the night.

"Take your positions," Ramiel instructed hurriedly. When both Julian and Marduk had one of their hands in the special-made leather loops sewn into Ramiel's fatigues, Ramiel kicked off the ground and rose into the air, taking his two friends with him. Gunshots still rang out beneath them as they skyrocketed, their enemies still seeking to kill them for their trespassing and theft, but the three men gave the bullets little heed.

They soared up into the night sky just as the stars came out of hiding, leaving the desert sands far behind them. And all was quiet and still once more.

Chapter Three

Brandi awoke to the violent sound of a fist pounding on her front door. She grumbled a curse and slowly, unsteadily got up from the bed. The knocking came again and she scowled as her head painfully pounded out the same rhythm. "I'm coming, I'm coming. Hold your horses," she called out, running her fingers through her long, tangled burgundy hair.

She opened the door and was surprised to see the Mt. Airy sheriff, Rob Adams, standing on her front porch. "Sheriff." She scratched her head and yawned sleepily. "What brings you here this morning?"

"It's not morning. It's one in the afternoon."

Brandi felt her eyes grow wide with her surprise. "Wow. It feels like morning. I guess it's because I didn't get much sleep last night." She yawned again.

"Yes, I know. That's why I came by here today."

Brandi heard an undercurrent of anger in the sheriff's voice and frowned. "What's going on?"

"I'll tell you what's going on. You scaring half the population of the town with your ghost stories and your fake video recordings, that's what's going on," he sputtered then seemed to collect himself, tamping down his obvious ire. "Do you know that after that stunt you pulled last night, the Marches are leaving town? Didn't you realize scaring them like that would have consequences?"

Brandi gritted her teeth. "I'm glad they're leaving. Their house is contaminated now. Moving is really the only foolproof way of protecting their remaining child."

"Look here, missy. You stay out of our way. We're on the trail of a serial kidnapper, not a goddamn monster straight out of your sick imagination."

"If you're looking so hard for this kidnapper, how come the FBI isn't involved? Wouldn't this situation fall under their jurisdiction, Sheriff?"

Rob scowled, face reddening. "Our town keeps to itself—we don't need strangers making things difficult for us. You know that as well as anybody else. So leave police business to us. In the meantime, you quit filling these poor people's heads with horror stories. I don't know why you're pulling this stunt, but it will go on no longer, do you understand me?"

"It's not a stunt," Brandi growled.

He ignored her. "Look, if I even hear a whisper about you taping more fake visits from this monster of yours, I'll bust your con-woman ass."

"I'm not a con-woman!" she exploded, completely losing her temper. "Now get the fuck off my porch."

His eyes blazed with anger. "I'll be watching you, missy. You keep that in mind the next time you try to scare off another family."

"Oh *whatever*." Brandi rolled her eyes and slammed the door in the sheriff's face. She watched through the peephole as he gathered himself, turned and left her porch. She listened for the sound of him getting in his patrol car. His door slammed and he revved the engine. She went to the window and watched as he turned the car around in her yard and gunned it down her driveway, spitting gravel in his wake.

Gritting her teeth against the urge to scream, she ran a hand through her tangled hair once more and released a sigh born of pure frustration. Walking through the cool house, she returned to her bedroom to gather up the clothes she would wear for the day. Her bedroom, nestled at the very back of the house, had once belonged to her nephew. But now, Brandi slept there.

Waiting.

Watching.

Just in case.

Brandi never slept at night, preferring instead to wait in her room full of video recording equipment and bright, motion-sensitive stage lights. Waiting for the monster. Nowadays she always slept a few hours after dawn had broken. It was all the rest she needed to keep going day after day.

Deciding to take a bath instead of a shower, Brandi turned on the water and went to check her equipment while the tub filled. She had both tape and digital video recorders set up and ready, facing the only closet in the house that wasn't boarded up. She removed last night's tape and put in another new one. Then she took the DVD out of the DVR and replaced that with a new DVD. Going over to her desk, tucked out of the way in a corner of the room, she slipped the night's media into the proper readers and went over them both in fast forward on her computer monitor.

Nothing.

Same as ever.

But one day, Brandi knew, if she was patient, she'd get something surely. And she would study it, as she studied all her recordings, and perhaps somehow she'd find a way to destroy the creature once and for all. Catching it where it had first manifested might yield different results from her other brushes with the monster. At least, she hoped it might. She really didn't know—and that scared her more than anything.

Brandi realized she was mad to tempt fate like this. The monster could just as easily take her as it did the children, or she at least suspected this was so. But she was determined to find a way to end the monster's reign of terror, no matter the cost to her own wellbeing.

She'd long ago given up on safety.

Brandi turned off her equipment and went to take her bath.

*****

Brandi enjoyed mowing the Dapplers' lawn every week. It gave her plenty of time to think and afforded her with some much-needed exercise. She knew she needed to lose a good thirty pounds before she'd be considered remotely healthy, but she rarely had the time to work the pounds off. So mowing the massive two-acre lawn of the Dappler family was the best way she knew to kill two birds with one stone.

She thought of her night with the Marches. She wondered if she could have done anything different to keep them from panicking like they had. She had shown them the tape of the monster, shaky and sometimes out of focus but clear enough to see that Brandi's stories of the beast were true. The Marches had been understandably distraught over the tape, terrified even. They'd immediately packed their bags and left with their daughter Emiline to find a hotel room for the remainder of the night.

They had left Brandi standing in the doorway of their house, completely forgetting her in their haste to leave. Brandi had used the opportunity to go back to the children's closet. She stepped into it and pushed aside the clothes that limply hung there, like tiny children-shaped skins. There was nothing but a wall behind the clothes. Brandi had suspected she would find no trace of the creature, no evidence of how he'd come to be there in the closet, but she had hoped that this time…maybe. She had turned from the closet in disgust and left the Marches' home with a heavy heart, locking up behind her as she went.

Brandi had always been a brooder by nature, escaping to her own thoughts for hours at a time, ignoring everyone else around her. Gail had always told her she needed to get out more, meet more people, have some fun. But Brandi wasn't a social butterfly. Had never been. Not like Gail. Brandi much preferred her own company most of the time.

At twenty-seven, Brandi now wondered if she'd ever break free of the life she'd begun leading some three years ago. Would she ever be able to walk away from this tainted town, to escape the monster forever?

No.

She couldn't walk away from this. Not until some resolution had been met. Not until she found a way to catch the monster and destroy it, or at least keep it from harming any more innocent lives. She couldn't leave the rest of the town's families at risk, no matter that most of them thought she was crazy. She wanted, no *needed*, to find a way to end the disappearances.

She held little hope that she'd find any of the children though. It pained her heart, but she knew deep down there wasn't much chance of her recovering those little lost lives. She wouldn't even begin to know where to look for them, if they were even alive to be found.

Brandi paused, killing the motor of the push mower, and wiped the sweat off her brow. She knew she'd left brown streaks of dirt and gasoline on her forehead, but she didn't care. There was no one in Mt. Airy she cared to look her best for. And she certainly didn't care if the Dapplers saw her in a state of dishabille. Hopefully her tired appearance might even induce her employers to pay her a little more money.

Hey, every little bit helped, right?

Brandi had learned in the last three years not to scoff at the charity of others. For if she did, she would starve. It was that simple. Besides, she *did* earn every penny of the money she made by doing plenty of chores for the townspeople, so the wages she was earning weren't really considered charity. At least not in the literal sense of the word. It didn't really matter, though, she'd take what she could get and be happy for it.

A bright flash of light made her squint her eyes. But there was no light, just that of the sun. The light was all in her mind. Then an image of the monster flashed before her and her head immediately felt as if it would explode. She felt a trickle of warmth above her upper lip and reached to touch it with her fingers. They came back bloodied and the blood trickled down her lips, onto her chin.

Another vision. When would they stop?

Brandi held her head back and pinched the bridge of her nose to stem the flow of blood. This wasn't the first time such a thing had happened to her, nor, she knew, would it be the last. She was well practiced at handling the physically painful visions by now.

She wondered, for what seemed the millionth time, if she had a brain tumor or something like it. Maybe that was why she had the visions.

But no.

Every time she had a vision there was another disappearance within a couple of days. Such a thing could not be coincidence, so it was doubtful there was a physiological reason for the visions. Brandi had never believed in magic when she was young, she'd always been too serious to entertain such flights of fancy. But now, all grown up, she had begun to believe in a great many things she used to shun. The visions, the monster, everything that had happened in the past three years had revealed a new world of horror to Brandi. A world with plenty of magic in it, and none of it good.

The bleeding slowed but her hands were covered in the stuff, skin sticky and stiff as it began to dry. The bright smell of copper filled her sinuses and the taste of it tortured her tongue. Her head ached as if a thousand pieces of glass were being stabbed into her skull. It would ache, she knew from experience, for the rest of the day.

The vision could only mean one thing. There would be another disappearance. And soon.

Brandi tried and failed not to throw up at the knowledge.

It would be a long time before she slept again. She knew the monster was coming. But where would it manifest this time? Brandi could only guess. It seemed her visions were only good for one thing—warning her of the monster's return, but yielding no information on how to prevent it.

Brandi wiped her mouth and wrapped her dirty, bloodstained hands around the handle of the mower and gripped it tightly. She wanted to tell someone, warn someone of what was about to happen. But the police would never believe her, and few, if any, of the townspeople would pay her warnings any heed. She was on her own.

And for once that scared the living shit out of her.

* * * * *

Atlanta, Georgia
One of the many Templar headquarters dotting the eastern United States.

Julian handed over the spear tip and watched as Gregori's eyes widened in astonishment. "You found it," he breathed.

Julian smiled. "Yes, my lord. It took many months of research but here it is at last, safe from harm and misuse."

Gregori, Julian's superior within the Templar and his very good friend, had tears in his eyes as he looked up from the spear. "I can't believe I'm holding this."

"Believe it. Now there are only two keys left to find. The good news about that is I've already been researching through the old records and I think I might know what the next key is."

"Tell me," Gregori commanded, immediately alert at Julian's words.

"I believe it is the Hope diamond, my lord." Though the title might have sounded archaic to any ears but their own, it was a show of Julian's deep respect that he continued to use it, even after all their years as friends.

Gregori frowned. "How did you find that out? Does the stone call to you as the other keys have?"

"It does. And I've read the legends surrounding the stone. How it was stolen from a Hindu idol, how it ruined the lives of everyone who touched it. The stone has great power, of that there can be no doubt. But it also dates back to the time of chaos, when the Earth first gave birth to life. There are ancient proverbs regarding the stone, and cave paintings that depict it in full detail. The stone is timeless and eternal. That fact, coupled with its incredible power and my sixth sense, have led me to believe that it is the next key we must acquire if we wish to save this world."

"How can you possibly acquire it? It is under constant guard, seen by hundreds of people every day. There is no way you can breach the security. It has never been done."

The corner of Julian's lip lifted in a wry smile. "Just because it hasn't ever been done, does not mean that it's an impossibility."

"And what if you do succeed in taking the stone, won't its curse befall you?"

"I will not touch it with my flesh. I believe that is what sparks the curse."

"And you are willing to risk it, Julian?"

"I am," he answered determinedly. "If I don't risk it, who will? The world is in a state of mounting danger. The keys must be found soon or I fear there will be no saving it."

Gregori nodded. "It's the truth you speak, my friend." His silver hair glinted in the florescent lighting. "Will you take Marduk and Ramiel with you again?"

"They wouldn't let me leave without them." Julian chuckled fondly. "Together we have fast become a formidable team. And good friends besides."

"To think that we Templars would become comrades with vampires and revenants and other creatures of darkness," Gregori sighed. "Times have truly changed, have they not, my friend?"

Julian nodded, but remained loyal in his next words. "Ramiel and Marduk have been invaluable to me on this quest for the seven keys. They are both good men, despite their handicaps."

"I'm not sure anymore that they are handicaps." Gregori shook his head. "And that is what scares me the most."

"Do I have your permission to go after the sixth key?"

"You truly believe it is the Hope diamond?"

"I do," Julian answered firmly.

"It may not fit its lock now. It has been cut down in size quite a lot, has it not?"

"We don't yet know how the locks will work. But I believe the lock will accommodate the changes in the stone."

"Then go," Gregori commanded. "Go with my blessing."

"Thank you, my lord."

Julian left the room, bowing respectfully to Gregori before departing. Outside Gregori's door, he ran smack into Marduk, who was waiting there for him expectantly. "Are we going to steal the diamond?" the smaller, darker man asked without missing a beat, falling into step beside Julian.

"I see no other way to procure it," Julian answered.

In Babylonian times, Marduk had been worshipped as a living god. The grace and nobility he carried with him always attested to this proud heritage. His wheat blond hair, a color very few Babylonians had ever seen, was full and rich, lying on his shoulders in bright, glossy radiance. His skin, a deep, dark bronze, kept him from seeming androgynous, but only just. His face was simply too pretty for a man. And if he stood still for too long, he looked like a living statue, something that often set Julian's nerves on end, much to his discomfort.

Marduk was a revenant. He had been sacrificed by his people to their god and then resurrected by the temple priests, granting him immortality. He had been kept as a religious icon for many long years, in the very same temple he had once built, as a living god. Julian had no idea how Marduk had escaped his homeland, or when, but he often saw the haunted look of one who had known much suffering hovering behind the amber eyes of his friend.

"It will not be easy," Marduk warned, bringing Julian's attention back to the present.

"I am well aware of that," Julian returned. He grinned. "As if that has ever stopped us before."

Marduk returned his smile. "I have often wondered what it would be like to be a jewel thief."

"You read too much fiction, my friend."

Marduk laughed. "I do. But I cannot help it. I love to read the words of today's peoples. Just as was true in my time, they hold a magic all their own, and are an excellent escape from the mundanity of life."

"Since when has your life ever been mundane, Marduk?"

"Good point," he said, chuckling.

"When night falls, we'll make our move on the Smithsonian."

"It's heavily guarded. There has never been a successful break-in, to my knowledge," Marduk warned.

Julian sighed. "I know, my friend. But where others have failed, we must succeed."

"At least you have the advantage of true immortality. You're virtually indestructible. If you promise to act as my shield, I guarantee you I'll get the diamond," Marduk teased.

Julian laughed and cuffed Marduk on the shoulder. "We all have the advantage of immortality, or have you forgotten?"

Marduk shook his head. "No, I haven't forgotten. But Ramiel and I can be killed, though I admit it would take much effort. You cannot die, no matter what is done to you, Templar Knight. You have drunk from the Grail. There is no danger to you, anywhere, not anymore."

"We have offered both you and Ramiel the chance to drink from the Grail," Julian pointed out.

Marduk shuddered imperceptibly. "I want nothing more to do with religious icons, no matter what religion it stems from. I've had enough of such things to last several lifetimes."

"And Ramiel doesn't want to take the chance that the power of the Grail might somehow smite him down."

"Ramiel is not evil, no matter what he thinks of himself. He is an honorable man…uh, vampire." Marduk grinned. "The Grail would not harm him. I'm sure of that much."

Julian nodded. "Well, if we're to be of any use tonight, I suggest we seek our chambers and take our rest. Tonight's quest will by no means be an easy one. We'll need all our wits about us."

Marduk agreed and they split ways, both going to different parts of the compound, seeking their beds and some much needed relaxation time.

Julian thought about the events to come, what might happen, what could happen. There were so many variables involved in such an endeavor as breaking into the Smithsonian. There was no telling what might happen. What might happen to anyone on his team.

It was a long time before Julian slept. And when he did, his dreams were filled with the vision of a small, lush woman with long, dark burgundy hair wrapping itself tight around his body like a vise.

Chapter Four

It was full dark and Brandi sat, waiting patiently, at the foot of her bed, staring intently at the closet door. The bright UV lights she had positioned around the room were motion activated, but Brandi was so still—and had been for a couple of hours now—that they remained dark for the time being. She didn't know why she had to undertake this ritual every night she spent in her sister's house, but she was compelled to keep doing it. Willing the monster to appear and…what? Would she suddenly know of a way to dispel the creature? So far she'd been out of luck on that score.

Brandi feared that in some dark corner of her mind she actually wanted the monster to take her. To take her to the same place as all those missing children. But the beast had never taken an adult before. Brandi wasn't even sure it could. And so, still, she waited, not knowing exactly what she was waiting for.

After her vision, she knew that the monster was sure to strike again, and soon. She'd had the same vision three times in the past two days—a record for her. She wondered, not for the first time, just how many nosebleeds she had experienced over the past three years due to these strange premonitions. More than she dared to count.

Seven children were now reported missing, and all of them, Brandi knew, had been the victims of the monster's hunger. Where the children went after the boogeyman took them, she couldn't guess. But she hoped fervently, with all her being, that the children were still alive somewhere, simply waiting to be found.

She didn't really believe that though, and she hated herself for it.

Brandi hated the haunted look in the eyes of those who had lost their babies. It racked her with such guilt that she couldn't do something to help these people. Especially for her sister and nephew. Gail had tried hard to make a go of it in Mt. Airy after Nick's disappearance, but in the end—just as many others now—she had left the town for good. Brandi called her once a week, just to keep tabs on how Gail and her husband and remaining child were doing, but a chasm had grown between them. One Brandi had no idea how to bridge.

Gail thought Brandi mad. Completely. And Brandi couldn't blame her, really. In some ways she guessed she was a little mad, after all. But that would end with the death of the creature that stalked the closets of children all throughout town. It had to, or else she was truly lost.

Exhausted yet still brimming with anxiety, Brandi began to doze off. The gray shapes in the darkness of the room mocked her, sending her into dreams that held many monsters and little hope. It had been so long since Brandi had been given the opportunity to sleep during the night. She knew, in the back of her mind, that she was making a mistake by going to sleep...but she couldn't fight it. She was under in a matter of seconds, oblivious to the world around her and the frights to be found laying in wait within it.

She awoke, many minutes later, to the faint sound of something moving within the closet. She blinked hard and focused her gaze on it, unmoving. The knob on the door turned and the UV lights flared, dispelling all darkness. Brandi jumped up from the bed and grabbed her baseball bat—even knowing as she did that it would never work on the monster—and approached the closet on catlike feet.

This was it. Finally.

The door burst open and she was thrown back with the force of the resulting wind. A black image appeared in the darkness of the closet, drawing nearer with each passing second. Brandi squinted in the light to see it—and was shocked to see what looked like a man, a black stocking mask concealing his identity, coming through the void that had become the back of the closet. The figure held his hands up in front of his face, as if the light blinded him.

Brandi regained her wits and swung the bat with all her might. She caught the man in the shoulder, surprising him and sending him sprawling. Something sparkled on a chain around his neck, nearly blinding her once more. She moved to swing again, aiming for his legs, but quick as lighting the man was up, regaining his feet. He ran from the room, breaking anything that happened to be in his way as he fled. Brandi gave chase, quick on her feet, but not half so quick as the retreating man.

"Stop! Who are you?" she shouted even as she sprinted to catch up.

The man had reached her front door. She followed him out onto the porch just in time to see him swiftly disappear within the thick, black trees of the surrounding woods. Brandi was barefoot, but she paid this fact little heed as she jumped down off the porch and took off at a dead run after her quarry.

The woods were quiet and secretive. Before, Brandi had always loved to take a stroll through the woods, but tonight the looming shadows of trees and bracken frightened her as she pursued the man in black. Branches slapped her face and caught in her unbound hair. Thorns bit at her ankles and legs, and her toes stubbed against dozens of roots and rocks protruding from the dirt. But still she ran on.

The man, she could barely see him now in the distance, was headed for the highway, which lay just beyond the woods. A thin veil of fog had drifted down—there were several creeks nearby—and her vision was handicapped because of it. She caught one more glimpse of the man in black before he disappeared in the darkness.

She ran on for several more minutes, following the direction she'd last seen the man heading. She made it to the highway at last, breathless and bleeding, but could see no sign of her quarry.

"Damn it!" she screamed, swinging her bat with frustrated rage. "What the hell just happened?" she asked the darkness, expecting and receiving no answer to her question. "What the hell?" The words ended on a whisper.

She didn't know. Nothing like this had ever happened before.

She turned in circles as if to catch sight of the man in black, but in her bones she already knew he was long gone.

"That wasn't the boogeyman," she murmured to herself, hugging her arms about her. "So then who or what was it?"

A man. It had to have been a man—he'd been clumsy and he'd run from her. But how had a man come through the closet? She'd checked the closet as the last rays of the sun had sank into the horizon, and she'd watched it all night. No one could have snuck into the closet without her knowledge.

He had come from the void.

The back of her closet had been missing, a black hole, nothing more—as was always the case when the monster came through. But there had been no monster. Just the man. How was that even possible?

Too many questions, and no answers to any of them, weighed heavily on her mind. She shook her head as if to clear it of cobwebs and turned, slowly going back through the midnight black woods from which she'd come. Her feet screamed in pain, as did her many other minor wounds, but she ignored them all by sheer force of will.

Unable to stop herself, she turned around and headed back to the highway once again. The town of Mt. Airy was quite small, so there was little traffic, even during rush hour. Now the long road was deserted. Not a car to be seen in either direction. She crossed the two lane highway and into the woods that lay on the other side. Not a sound broke the silence, not a leaf stirred. There was no man in black.

Had he even existed, or had her mind played an elaborate trick on her?

Growling, she turned and left once more. It took her several long minutes to make her way back, even at a brisk walk on her aching feet. When she saw the lights of the house up ahead, she stopped and frowned.

What had just happened? Had she slept? Had this all been a dream? Here she was in the woods, barefoot and disheveled. Had she simply been sleepwalking? Brandi felt frustrated tears well up in the corner of her eyes because, quite simply, she didn't know the answers to her own questions.

Had she finally gone mad, as everyone already suspected her of being?

Brandi brushed the tears angrily away—she hated any sign of weakness in herself—and went to sit on the front porch swing. This was the best place for her to think as she rocked slowly back and forth in the mild night air. She was afraid, for the moment, of going back inside the house. She didn't know what, if anything, she'd find there.

But wait. The videotapes.

She shot to her feet, ignoring the pain, and ran into the house. Brandi grabbed the tape and DVD from the video cameras with shaking hands and set them to play through her computer. She skipped to the moment when she was sure the incident with the man in black had occurred. She had a perfect view of the closet door for several long seconds then...static.

Static? *Static!* Brandi hit the side of her monitor, as if by doing so it would make the blurry picture go away. It didn't. For all of three minutes there was nothing on the tape or the DVD. The video cameras had both failed to record those three simultaneous minutes. After the static, the image of the closet manifested and it seemed that the recording devices had begun working again.

At the same time.

What the hell was going on?

"I have no idea," she answered in a shaken whisper that echoed eerily in the silent room and in her head.

* * * * *

Getting into the Smithsonian National Museum of Natural history would be difficult, even for three men with extraordinary talents.

None of them could simply walk through the walls of the great building that housed the diamond, not like some of the other members of the Templar society. But they did have other ways of getting in.

Ramiel approached the two massive metal doors and studied the locks intently. "Give me a few minutes, gentlemen, and I'll have you inside."

Ramiel's body blurred then disappeared, leaving only a thick mist behind. That mist turned in the air for a moment then flew to the crease of the door jamb. It disappeared through the miniscule gap, leaving Julian and Marduk standing outside the doors. Several long minutes passed and nothing happened.

"Maybe he's having trouble with the motion sensors," Marduk remarked.

"I don't think so." Julian shook his head.

Inside, Ramiel let his incorporeal form drift up to the motion sensors placed randomly about the room. He gathered moisture that would have formed in his mouth if he weren't a nebulous vapor and used it to short the electronic circuits in the sensors, effectively disabling them.

But then...a guard appeared at the other end of the great room. Ramiel fled to the shadows, hiding. The guard looked around, staying well away from the scope of the motion sensors, and moved on. Ramiel breathed a sigh of relief and came out of hiding after waiting a few more minutes just to be sure no one else was coming.

Ramiel took his physical form once more and stood before the great doors of the museum. There was a security keypad by the door. He touched it with his forefinger, sending a bolt of electricity to the keypad, frying its insides. Ramiel only hoped it was now disabled. He took a deep breath and disengaged the locks, one by one. Then, still looking about for the guards, he opened the door to his friends.

Thankfully, no alarm sounded.

"It's about time," Marduk whispered.

"Shh, make no sound," Ramiel cautioned. "There are human guards about the place."

"Then we'll have to be extra careful, won't we," Julian noted.

"What floor is the diamond on?" Marduk asked.

"The second," Julian answered, immediately moving toward the stairs that would lead them to the upper floors. "Come now, and be silent," he commanded in a hushed whisper.

The trio made their way up the stairs, ever vigilant, like shadows in the dim light. It was a great risk they were taking, but a necessary one; one they all believed in wholeheartedly. The seven keys had to be found, and soon. The veils between the worlds were tearing, allowing many evils straight from the Pit to wander the Earth unchecked.

After a good half hour of searching, dodging guards and avoiding additional motion sensors, they finally found the diamond. Illuminated by the lights in its display case, it cast a rainbow of color bright enough to blind and Ramiel winced, hanging back away from it, as if its brightness pained him.

It very probably did, Julian realized with little surprise.

Julian approached the case, reaching out his hand as if to touch the stone. He stopped abruptly and frowned, tilting his dark head to the side as if listening to something only he could hear.

"I don't feel anything," Julian said at last. "I should feel its pull, but I do not."

"Strange. Perhaps we were wrong. Perhaps the stone isn't the sixth key after all," Ramiel said softly.

Marduk came forward and looked at the stone. He studied it for a long while then looked at Julian, disappointment evident in his amber eyes. "That stone isn't real."

Julian blinked in surprise. "What? Not real? How can that be?" he exploded.

Marduk shrugged. "Be quiet," he warned. "I don't understand it. But I've seen many jewels in my time and I know that this stone is paste, fake, nothing more than an imposter. You can tell by the inclusions deep within, flaws, which are invisible to the naked eye. This stone was handmade. A very clever fake."

Julian was stunned. "How can this be so?"

"I don't know. I only know that this is *not* the Hope diamond," Marduk answered.

"I don't understand," Julian breathed. "Has it always been fake?"

Marduk thought for a moment then shook his head. "I've seen it on television, the real stone, so I don't think this imposter has been here long. No, this is the work of someone else."

"How will we be able to find it now?" Ramiel raged.

"*Shh!* There are still guards about," Marduk warned once more.

"The keys have called to me over the years," Julian murmured. "This stone will call to me as well, no matter where it may now be. Come, let us be gone from this place before we are noticed."

"What will we do now?" Marduk asked.

"We will wait and see where the stone leads us," Julian answered. "In the meantime, we'll begin our search for the seventh key."

"Let's hope it's easier to find than the diamond," Ramiel growled.

The men left the building the way they had come, leaving behind no trace of their presence but for the ruined motion sensors and security keypad. It was a long time before any of them had anything more to say.

* * * * *

Brandi sat watching the news without really seeing the television. Her thoughts were miles away, far removed from the story of a break-in at the Smithsonian.

She wondered if, in fact, she had gone crazy at last.

She hadn't slept in four days, not since the incident with the man in black. Insomnia was no stranger to her, especially in these last three years, but this was a little different. She couldn't go to sleep, not even a doze, no matter how hard she tried—her mind was a storm cloud of thoughts thundering in her head. Brandi couldn't help it, but she was now beginning to believe that perhaps she was as loony as the people of Mt. Airy thought she was.

How had a man stepped through the closet? How was it even possible? Was it magic? Was it something else? Brandi didn't know. There were no answers to her questions, at least none that she could find.

Now Brandi lay on her couch before the television, gray eyes red and swollen, so tired she felt she could sleep for days if only the insomnia would go away. She lifted a Twinkie to her mouth—her favorite lazy food—and took a large, satisfying bite. Screw her weight problem; this business with the man in black was much more pressing and besides, she needed the sugar to think clearly.

The phone rang.

Brandi fumbled for the handset positioned on an end table just behind her head. "Hello," she slurred into the receiver.

"Brandi, it's Brooke Baily."

Brandi sat up on the couch, rising so fast that the blood rushed from her head.

"Hello, Brooke. How is everything?" Brandi swallowed hard in preparation for what she knew was to come next.

Brooke began crying into the phone. "Elizabeth has been taken," she said in a rush of jumbled words.

Brandi didn't know how to respond. "Did you call the police?" she asked helplessly.

"Yes, of course. She went missing last night. The cops were here until about ten minutes ago."

"Why have you called me, then?" Brandi asked, already knowing the answer.

"Brandi, honey, I never thought you were crazy. There's too much unexplained stuff in the world for me to be judgmental. You know that don't you?"

Brandi nodded, even though she knew Brooke couldn't see it. "I know you didn't believe the rumors. I know that's why you let me do some odd jobs for your family—which I greatly appreciate."

Brooke Baily took a deep, shaky breath. "I want to see what the others have seen. I want you to show me what took my daughter from me."

With a deep sigh, Brandi weakly put her hand to her head. For once, she didn't think she had the strength to meet the monster, tired and demoralized as she was. But Brooke had had the courage to call her; it was only fair that Brandi do for her what she had now done for seven others. "I'll show you what I've videotaped from the others. But I don't know if I can do more than that. You don't have any more children who might lure the monster back, so I doubt you could see it firsthand."

"Please try," Brooke pleaded.

"All right. If I can, I'll show you," Brandi promised. "I'll be there tonight, at sundown."

"We'll be waiting for you," Brooke sobbed again and the sound almost broke Brandi's heart. "Thank you so much, Brandi."

"I don't need your thanks, Brooke. Besides, after tonight, you'll probably hate me for what I'm going to show you."

"I won't hate you," Brooke vowed.

Brandi bowed her head. "We'll see," she answered. "I'll come to you tonight, Brooke."

"Bless you. Goodbye."

Brandi stared at the phone as if it were a snake. She hated the fear, the sorrow and even the determination she had heard in Brooke's shaken voice. Brooke might not think now that her life will change after tonight, might assume she could go on with her life with only an aching heart for her lost daughter. The sight of the boogeyman would likely scar her forever and eventually, if not immediately, she would blame Brandi for showing her such a horror. It was inevitable.

Regardless, Brandi knew she owed it to Brooke to show her the truth. The woman had been more than kind to her over the past three years. It was the very least she could do in payment for that kindness.

Brandi only hoped she had the strength left to face the boogeyman once again.

She lay back down on the couch and willed herself to sleep, to regain some strength to get her through the night ahead. It was a long time in coming, but at last she was able to doze. It wasn't real sleep, but she would take what she could get and be happy.

At least until sundown.

Chapter Five

Brandi walked across the lawn of the Baily house, holding her video camera in one hand and her flashlight in the other. It was a warm night, humid and filled with the thick, cloying perfume of blooming honeysuckle. She had walked the two miles from her house to the Bailys', despite her need to conserve what strength she had. She had desperately needed the time to think up a way to make it through the night and all it had in store for her.

For once, Brandi was at a loss. On the one hand she was questioning her very sanity, on the other she was determined to ferret out this evil specter and face it. The two contradicting emotions confused and weakened her. Something she could ill afford if she was to make it through the night. She walked up the steps of the Bailys' porch and heaved a heavy sigh of exhaustion, steadying her nerves as best she could in the few serene moments left to her.

Brooke answered the door before Brandi could even press the doorbell.

"Brandi, come in." Brooke stepped aside, allowing her to enter. "I'm so glad you're here."

"Sorry I'm late. I walked. Where is Elizabeth's room?" Brandi said the words in a rush, her body and mind already gearing up for the ordeal ahead.

Brooke led her deeper into the house, looking over her shoulder every few seconds as if to reassure herself that Brandi was following her.

"In here." Brooke motioned to a door papered with posters and childlike drawings.

Brandi walked through the door into Elizabeth's disheveled room. She immediately went to the closet, opened it up and looked inside. Nothing. Only some clothes and toys scattered about, in a mess that only a child could make sense of. Brandi turned to Brooke, who waited fretfully by the door. "I'll need you to leave," Brandi told her softly.

"Can't I stay and watch?"

"I'm not sure the monster will come with so many adults in the room. I've never tried it." In actuality, she wasn't sure Brooke could handle the shock of seeing the monster firsthand, not in the state she was in now. "I don't even know if it will come tonight at all. I've got my camera," she held up the video recorder, "if something happens I'll get it all on tape. You can count on it."

Mr. Baily, a forty-ish man of average height with sad, soulful brown eyes, came up behind his wife. He looked rough, as if he hadn't slept in a long while. "Let's leave her alone," he said, rubbing Brooke's shoulders. "Let her do what she came here to do."

Brooke nodded and turned into the waiting arms of her husband, closing the door softly behind them as they left.

Alone, Brandi closed the closet door and sat on the floor in front of it. She sat on her knees, so that if the monster came she could immediately shoot to her feet. She didn't expect the creature to return. But she could be wrong. There could be no missed chances here, so she held a small hope that the beast would show itself once more.

Brandi tried not to let the sight of lonely toys and teddy bears ruin her concentration, but her mind wandered despite her determination. The room seemed a little lost, cut adrift, without a child playing in it. Toys were haphazardly strewn about, as if the child had left only seconds ago, and the room still held a faint trace of the scent of baby shampoo. The perfume made Brandi's heart swell with sadness.

What was she to do? She couldn't kill the monster. She could only watch as it took child after child, again and again. She was as helpless as every other parent in town. When would it all end? She wished fervently that she had an answer to that question. For now, she would do the only thing she could do. She would wait for the creature to show itself.

Hours ticked by. How many, Brandi didn't know, but her legs were numb from being tucked under her for so long. She thumped her fists against her thighs to wake them up and thousands of tiny, stabbing needles ate at her from her feet to her knees.

"Come on," she said impatiently, running her fingers through her hair in a nervous gesture. She glared at the closet door as if that would help hurry the creature along.

The doorknob rattled.

Brandi jumped to her tingling feet, startled but determined to stand her ground.

The knob turned slowly.

Brandi raised the camera and hit record. This was it.

The door opened, letting a blast of cold air into the room. Out from the darkness came the shadow of the monster, coming at her so fast she didn't have time to react. It loomed before her, taking on a humanoid shape, reaching its long, alien arms out to her.

A sense of great sorrow and fear assailed her; the monster fairly reeked of it. It was all Brandi could do not to throw up. She tightened her fingers on the camera until her knuckles were bone white. Hopelessness took her in a cold rush and for the first time, Brandi felt like giving up. Like just letting go, letting the monster have its way. The monster reached for her and she faltered, the smoky hand barely passing by her face, and Brandi leaned into it against her will, following it back toward the closet. Her head swam with visions of thousands of screaming children. Tears leaked out of her eyes. She couldn't find the strength to turn on her flashlight. This was finally it.

The bedroom door splintered and flew wide, slamming back on its hinges. A man in a long black coat sprinted into the room, his presence so commanding that for a moment Brandi forgot the monster entirely. He drew a five-foot sword from within the coat's voluminous folds, brandished it with elaborate movements—he was obviously well used to fighting with this sword—and stabbed at the monster. The blade glowed white, brighter than a star. The light touched the boogeyman and it screamed, shying away. The man twirled and brought the sword down upon what should have been the neck of the beast.

The shadow dispersed, like a black mist being sucked back to where it had come from. In the blink of an eye, the back of the closet became visible again and the man sheathed his weapon with deft movements, making it disappear into his coat as if by magic.

He turned to her, his icy blue eyes pinning her to the spot. "What in all the hells were you trying to do here, woman? Have you any idea of the danger you have placed yourself in?"

Brandi blinked. "Who the fuck are you?" was all she could think to say.

The man closed the gap between them and swiped her camera straight out of her hand. He shoved the camera under her nose threateningly. "Do you think these toys will protect you? They will not. You are playing with things that you do not understand!"

Anger replaced shock and Brandi felt her cheeks grow warm. "Who the hell are you and what makes you think you can talk to me like this, buddy?" she thundered.

The man gritted his teeth. She actually heard them grinding behind his square jawline.

It was then that Brandi noticed the distraught forms of Brooke and her husband standing in the doorway. She felt like the worst fiend that she couldn't find any words to make their horror any less horrible to bear. But she was too shaken and angry to think straight.

"My god," Brooke said. "I saw it. I can't believe it, but I saw it! Was that thing real? How could that thing be real?" Her voice turned shrill on those last words.

Brandi nodded mutely before sliding her eyes back to the stranger with the cold blue gaze. He too was looking at the Bailys but the moment her eyes touched him, he turned his attention back to her. He frowned at her and, still more than a little angry, Brandi scowled back at him.

"We need to talk," the man said, his voice deep and rich, with more than a trace of a French accent, and grabbed her by the upper right arm. He practically dragged her over to the stunned Bailys. The man reached in his pocket and pulled out a thick wad of money. "For your doors," he said, handing the money to the still stunned Brooke. "And board up that closet," he told them as he passed, not bothering to slow down. He didn't stop until they were out on the lawn in the dark.

Brandi couldn't help but notice the front door had been busted through as well, wood splintered everywhere as if it had exploded inward.

"What's your name, woman?" the man asked.

Brandi sneered. "I'm not giving you my name until you give me yours," she fired back belligerently.

The man sighed heavily, his incredibly wide shoulders drooping somewhat. "My name is Julian. Now give me your name, unless you wish me to continue calling you 'woman' or simply 'hey you'." His shoulders straightened, as if he was preparing himself for a battle.

Brandi was just mad enough that she might give him one. "I'm Brandi."

"Brandi, do you know how much danger you placed yourself in tonight?"

She rolled her eyes. "I've done this many times. I've got a flashlight—the light scares it away. I was in no danger."

"The bogle can just as easily take adults as it can children."

"No, it can't," she retorted, but she didn't really believe her own words. "It's never taken an adult."

"That's because it prefers to feed off the innocence of children. But that does not mean it cannot take you, should it choose to. Should you force it to with your foolish gamble."

"I can take care of myself," she growled. "I've been doing this for three years. I think I'm safe enough from the…what did you call it? Bogle? Anyway, I wasn't in any danger." She wondered, in the back of her mind, if that were really true. But she would never have admitted it to him.

"You do not understand your position here. You were deliberately luring the monster to come to you. You were calling to it. Why? What purpose does that serve?"

Brandi pointed at the Bailys' house. "They lost their child because of this damn thing. I was only trying to show them—"

"Did you think they really needed to see?"

She felt as if she'd been struck. He had echoed the same thoughts she'd been worrying over for the past three years. "They wanted to see the truth. They deserved to see if it they wanted to."

"No one wants to see something like that." His blue eyes blazed, even in the darkness. "They had no idea of what they were getting into, and you should have known better."

"Wait, just what are *you* doing here?" she sputtered. "Do you know the Bailys or something, because I've never seen you and I know everyone in this town. How do you know so much about the boogeyman—your *bogle*—huh?"

The man simply looked at her for a long, tense moment, his gaze never leaving hers. Unwavering. "I came…" He shook his head then as if to clear it, putting the palm of his hand against his head. "I came here to find something."

"I don't understand you," she said when he didn't offer to say more.

"You don't need to," he said, regaining his composure and grabbing her arm again. He pulled her along behind him across the lawn toward where a sleek, black motorcycle waited. "I barely understand it myself," he grumbled.

"Quit— *Oof!*" She stumbled, bending her ankle painfully. She would have fallen if he hadn't been gripping her arm so tight. "Let go of me, you fucking freak!" She swatted at his hand, noting how big and brutishly strong it was as he continued to drag her along. She tried and failed not to notice other, more disconcerting details about him.

He was much taller than her, by at least a foot. His glossy, dark, chocolate brown hair was long, reaching well past his shoulders, secured with a piece of rawhide at the nape of his neck. His face was a work of art, as if carved from stone, strong and square and hard. His throat was thick with corded muscle and a tribal tattoo ran from the side of it down into the black shirt he wore beneath his coat. The shirt fit him like a second skin, displaying his heavily muscled chest and tight abs. His coat was straight from neck to waist, then it flared out like a skirt—a deacon's coat—around his long, long legs. He wore calf-length black boots with shiny silver buckles all over them that glinted brightly in the moonlight.

He was breathtaking. Like some dark warrior straight from a fairy tale.

They made it to the motorcycle and Julian stopped dragging her, instead turning her to face him. His eyes, Brandi noted, were more than just an icy blue. They were pale blue— nearly silver—with a darker rim of blue surrounding the bright iris and the rim of his pupil. His lashes were long and thick, black as midnight. He had the sort of eyes any woman would kill for. Sultry witch eyes.

He studied her just as closely as she studied him, his gaze taking in all of her from head to toe. "I didn't expect this at all," he growled under his breath, speaking as if he'd forgotten she was even there, but Brandi knew he hadn't forgotten. His eyes positively drank her up.

"What?" she prodded.

His gaze flashed to hers blankly. "What?"

"What didn't you expect?" she asked in mounting exasperation.

He shook his head and closed his eyes, sighing heavily. "Nothing. It's nothing. Come on, I'll take you home." He threw his long leg over the motorcycle and started the motor, which rumbled like a giant awakening from a deep slumber.

"Wait! I don't want to leave the Bailys until I've explained everything—"

"Don't worry about the Bailys. They'll work things out for themselves. Now get on." His tone suggested he would brook no more refusals.

Brandi had never ridden on a motorcycle. She wasn't sure she wanted to. But she wasn't about to turn chicken in front of this virile, commanding man. No way. She shrugged, gathered her courage and swung her own leg over the motorcycle, her chest coming to rest against Julian's broad back. Her legs cradled his hips and the vibration of the motorcycle moved her sensually against him. Intimacy in this position was unavoidable. Brandi felt her cheeks burn with her embarrassed discomfort.

He revved the engine and peeled rubber, tires screaming loudly, turning the bike around and heading back down the Bailys' driveway. Once they reached the main road, he sped up until the wind was biting at their exposed skin. His long coat tails flapped in the wind on either side of her, like the wings of some great bat. Brandi threw her arms around Julian's waist, buried her face against his back and hung on for dear life.

The wind toyed with Brandi's long hair, whipping it about until it was a wild tangle. The bike vibrated between her legs, throwing off what little concentration she had left.

With her face buried against him as they rode, she caught his scent and breathed it deep. He smelled of Nag Champa incense. His very skin exuded the fragrance. Delicious. She'd never before smelled a man with a better scent than this one, she was certain. His scent permeated her senses, making her head reel dizzily. She fought the urge to rub her face against his back and purr like a well-satisfied kitten.

Her primal reaction to the nearness of this man shocked and appalled her. She'd never had such a strong response to a total stranger. It almost scared her, it was that strong and immediate.

She felt him pressed against her, from her cheek resting against the hair that fell down his back to her loins, thighs and legs. He left her with no secrets to hide behind. If she felt him this intensely, she knew he, too, had to be aware of *her*, of her thighs surrounding his hips and her breasts pressed so tight against his broad back.

They came to a stop sign by the road and Brandi was afforded the opportunity to pull away from him a little.

"Which way?" he asked over his shoulder.

"That way." She pointed then grabbed his shoulder as he whipped the bike around the corner, tires squealing.

"Do you have to drive like this?" she shouted at him.

"Shut up and let me think," he barked back.

She felt her eyes go wide. Shut up? Had he actually told her to shut up? She had the wild urge to just start screaming, if only to see what he would do. But his impressive shoulder muscles flexed tautly and she thought better of it.

A few more turns and Brandi directed him down the long gravel drive that would lead to her house. She wasn't sure she was comfortable with this man knowing where she lived, but there was nothing for it. They were already here.

"Hang on," he said over the roar of the wind. "The ride's about to get bumpy."

Instead of slowing the bike down to accommodate the pits and bumps in the road, as she expected, he sped up dramatically. The ride became a wild roller coaster, with the wind roaring in her ears, but Julian easily controlled the growling machine despite the roughness of the terrain. It was actually quite impressive.

They came to a halt at the front steps of her porch, a dust cloud rising up behind them. Julian was the first one off the bike and he gallantly helped Brandi off with a hand at her elbow, but he didn't so much as look at her. His eyes seemed far away, as if he were deep in thought. She ignored the slight and tried instead not to let his touch affect her. But it was as futile an effort as neglecting to breathe. Something about him just got under her skin. That, coupled with his strangeness and her lack of sleep, threw her completely off guard. She had no clue how to handle this situation, none at all.

"Invite me in for a drink," he commanded, startling her.

"Buddy, you've got some gall, bossing me around like this," she growled.

He blinked slowly at her, his bright blue eyes burning like stars. "Regardless of your willingness, I *am* coming in. We have much to discuss."

Brandi felt her stubbornness rise to the rescue. "Why don't we discuss things out here?"

"Because I want to talk inside."

Brandi surprised herself by letting out a bark of laughter at his arrogant, overbearing manner. She shook her head and sobered quickly. "I don't want to invite you in," she continued to protest.

"I don't care," he shot back.

She gritted her teeth. "Fine. Stay out here on the porch then, I'm going in to catch some shuteye." *If I can*, but she didn't utter that part aloud.

He followed her to the door, hot on her heels, so close she could feel the warmth radiating from him at her back. With her hand on the doorknob, she turned to face him. "What do you think you're doing?"

"Lady, there's no reason to be obtuse about this," he said with an obvious show of patience.

She felt her eyes go wide with shock. "Me? *Obtuse*? Look, you twit, I don't even know you. No way am I inviting you into my house. You could be an axe murderer for all I know. Not to mention that you have a gigantic sword hidden in your coat somewhere!"

Julian reached into his coat and retrieved the sword. Brandi stepped back with a gasp as it winked at her in the moonlight, its earlier bright shine dimmed. "You mean this?" he asked. "Why don't I just leave it out here on the porch, does that make you feel safer?"

She eyed his tall, thickly muscled form and snorted. "No."

He grinned, a self-satisfied bearing of his bright white teeth, and he deftly tucked the sword back into his coat. "Go inside, Brandi."

"No."

Julian growled, moved swiftly and picked her up by the back collar of her blouse. Brandi shrieked as her feet dangled. He tightened his grip and she was almost choked by her shirt. "We'll go in together," he said and kicked in her door. He seemed adept at doing that.

He practically tossed her into the living room, he let go of her so suddenly, and she stumbled. He raised his hand and she winced, waiting for a blow, but he ran his hand through his hair instead, dislodging it from its band, and she let out a relieved sigh.

The blue of his eyes nearly glowed. He raised his hand again and looked at her. "You thought I was going to strike you," he accused.

Brandi didn't think to lie. "Yeah," she answered.

He shook his head. "Our paths have no doubt crossed for a reason. Now I am pledged to protect you. On my honor, I swear to you that I shall never hurt you if you don't deserve it," he said wryly. When she attempted to interrupt, he held up his hand and said, "Okay, okay, okay, I will not hurt you at all. On my honor, I so swear it." He winked at her boldly and she tried and failed to be unaffected by that sultry look.

She snorted again to hide her discomfiture. "Like I'm going to believe in the honor of someone I just met. Forget it."

He growled, eyes darkening dangerously. Brandi felt her pulse double its beat. "The last man who questioned my honor died a swift death."

Brandi laughed, then, seeing that Julian was completely serious, she doubled over with more. "You're a real peach, you know that?" she said, sobering with some effort. "You actually look as if you're telling me the truth. All right. Let's talk, big boy."

Chapter Six

Brandi's home was airy and spacious but Julian's thickly muscled body seemed to fill it, cramping the space, towering over her as she went to the kitchen to grab a glass of milk.

"I have questions that need to be answered," he said as she sat on a tall stool at the kitchen island in the middle of the room.

"Yeah, well, I've got some of my own," she shot back after taking a long swig of milk.

"Me first," he said, taking a seat opposite her.

"No way, this is my house. My questions first, then yours later. If you behave yourself."

He looked dumbfounded for a moment then completely schooled his features so that Brandi had no idea what he was thinking. "Fine," he said tersely. "We'll answer your questions first. What would you know from me?"

"Who are you?"

"I told you, I am Julian—"

"No. Not your name. *Who* are you, why are you here? How did you know about the boogeyman? I want to know everything. Spill it."

He eyed her for a minute and she wondered if he would refuse to answer her questions. Then he sighed and reached for her glass of milk, taking his own big gulp before speaking.

"I cannot tell you much but that I have had some experience with bogles in the past. When I was driving through tonight, I felt the presence of one near. I was led to the house, where you were calling the bogle out, and decided to take action before someone was hurt."

It didn't sound like the *whole* truth, but Brandi believed he was telling her some of it, and she nodded her head, letting the matter pass. "You know a lot about the boogeyman?"

"The bogle, yes."

"Have you seen him before?" she asked, curious.

"Not him, *it*. I have seen many in my time," he answered.

Brandi pondered that for a moment. "So our town isn't the only one plagued by this thing? There are others?"

"How is your town plagued by it?" he countered with a frown.

"Seven..." She shook her head, counting silently. "No. *Eight* children have disappeared in the past three years. All of them were taken by the boogeyman, the bogle, whatever it is."

Julian gaped, listening to her words with incredulity. "So many. I've never known of a bogle taking so many. They often visit town after town, taking one child here and there, but no more. This is most unusual."

"Yeah, well, welcome to my world." She poured another glass of milk.

"So this bogle has been here for three years?"

"Yeah. The first person to disappear was my nephew." She took a long drink, gathering the right words. "I'd been visiting for the weekend and I heard him scream in the middle of the night. I went to check on him, thinking it was just a bad dream, but his bedroom door seemed sealed shut. I couldn't get in. Nick screamed again and I panicked, beating against the door, running and slamming my body into it. Finally the wood splintered—I was so pepped up with adrenaline that I was stronger than I normally would have been—and when I opened the door, I saw him being dragged by some massive black form, straight into the open closet. I ran to stop it, but the closet door slammed shut in my face and when I opened it up, they were both gone."

"When did you encounter it next?"

"I waited for it in Nick's bedroom. Sure enough, the next night, the bastard came out again. I had a baseball bat—stupid, I know—and I beat at it, but the bat just went straight through the monster as if it were made of smoke. I panicked as the monster gathered itself and made a dive for me. I did the first thing that came to mind. I rushed to turn the lights on—"

"And the bogle disappeared," Julian finished for her, his French lilt leaving a faint trace in his words. "You were lucky. A bogle can just as easily take an adult, should it choose to." He echoed his earlier words.

Brandi shuddered. "I didn't know that. But it doesn't matter. The monster has never been close enough to lay a hand on me."

"What about tonight? I saw you leaning into the spirit," he reminded her. "It had you mesmerized."

She blushed. "I haven't slept in a few nights. I wasn't quite aware of what I was doing."

"You were fortunate that I came when I did. The beast almost had you."

Brandi looked at his proud face. He really was an attractive man—if one liked giant brutes, which she sort of did. He was at least six-five, maybe taller. He was thick with muscle from his tattooed neck down to his ankles, much like a bodybuilder. The coat he wore fit his body to perfection, accentuating his broad shoulders and narrow waist as it hugged his upper body before flaring around his legs. He was all man, from head to toe. He had a square jaw and a straight, narrow nose. He had high, proud cheekbones. His eyes were piercing from behind arched black brows, and his hands… Brandi shivered. His hands were strong and broad and long-fingered. Beautiful.

She wondered, for one brief and terrifying second, if he might be the man who'd come running out of her closet. But then she realized he was far taller and far more muscular than the man in the black mask had been, and she let it go.

"I would have turned on the flashlight, given a few seconds," she said at last.

"You didn't have a few seconds left," he pointed out. "It was but a couple of inches away from you."

Brandi couldn't argue with that. For a moment she herself had feared she was too late to fight the monster off. She'd just been so tired.

It occurred to her that she hadn't been the least bit sleepy since Julian had thrown himself between her and the bogle. She shrugged the strangely uncomfortable thought away and concentrated instead on her half empty glass of milk.

"Any more questions?" he asked.

"How do you know about the boogeyman in the first place?"

He gritted his teeth.

"You know, you'll damage your teeth if you keep doing that," she couldn't help but point out.

He ignored her. "I am part of a group that makes it a point to know all things about the netherworld. Bogles are a part of that. I've studied them extensively. As well as other, darker things."

Brandi just stared, dumbfounded. "You mean there are worse things than this monster? I don't believe you," she managed at last. "I can't."

"Believe it. And hope that you never learn firsthand how true that is."

"So you're, what, a paranormal investigator?"

He chuckled and the sound rolled over her like a warm wave. "I guess you could call it something like that. Now," he put both his arms on the table and clasped his hands together, "are you finally through with your questions?"

"For now," she snapped, busy fighting against his pure animal magnetism.

"What's your last name, Brandi?"

"It's Carroll."

"And who are your family? Names please," he added.

Brandi frowned, unsure of where he was going with these questions. "I have a half sister; her name is Gail."

"What about your parents?" he probed. "And their parents."

"They passed about five years ago. I was twenty-two." She didn't know why she added that last part. She felt herself blush. "But their names were Ron and Brenda. I never knew my grandparents—they had all died by the time I came along."

He took out a small, well-worn pad of paper and wrote it down the details. "Do you and your sister share the same father or mother?"

"Mother."

He wrote that down as well.

She frowned. "Look, just what are you doing?"

"There is some information I must obtain before going further."

"Before going further *where*?" she asked in growing exasperation.

"I can't say yet. But you'll be the first person to know." His bright eyes roved over her face, as if he were taking in every feature and memorizing it. "Trust me." He grabbed the glass of milk away from her and drank the remainder. He set the glass down and rose from his seat.

"Help yourself," she said sarcastically.

"I have to go now. But I warn you, behave tonight. Do not go baiting the bogle again. Let it rest."

Brandi was incredulous. No one had dared to tell her to behave since she was ten years old. "Who. The hell. Do you think you are?" she enunciated with biting fierceness.

He bent toward her. His breath smelled like cinnamon and Brandi tried valiantly not to breathe the scent deep into her lungs. He grabbed her chin and forced her to meet his gaze. "I am someone who knows better. Do not play with this bogle. Got it?" He released her abruptly.

She had every intention of doing the same thing she did every night—wait for the boogeyman to come straight through her nephew's closet. But Brandi didn't tell him that. Something warned her that he might take drastic measures to ensure that she "behaved". What those measures were, she didn't care to speculate.

"Fine. I've got it," she lied easily.

He looked at her hard for a long moment, and Brandi wondered if he just might go ahead and somehow make sure she followed his command. Then he nodded once, curtly, and left the kitchen. Brandi jumped down from her stool and followed him to the front door.

"Well, I'd like to say it was nice meeting you, but I don't really think it was," she said with some agitation at his retreating back.

He turned to her and pierced her with his gaze. "We'll meet again," he promised in a dark tone that made her shiver from head to toe.

He left her standing on her doorstep, dumbfounded. He jumped on his motorcycle and drove away before she could think of any sort of reply. They would meet again? God, she hoped she had her wits about her when they did. It wouldn't do to go drooling all over the man each time she saw him. She needed to get a grip on herself. She sighed and went back into the house, not even bothering to try to close her broken door, instead leaving it wide open.

It was turning out to be a very, very long night.

* * * * *

Now biding the time in their Atlanta headquarters, Marduk and Ramiel were in the practice room, using Bo staves to fight each other. Both men were lightning quick and deft with their weapons, never once connecting the wooden poles with the other's flesh.

"Come join us," Ramiel said in that strange, melodious voice of his. He hadn't looked at Julian, but Julian knew he could smell his approach. Ramiel's senses were phenomenally overdeveloped.

Julian, needing to blow off some steam after meeting the very volatile, very delicious-looking Brandi, took his own staff and entered the fray. The three men circled each other, sizing up one another. Marduk struck first, coming at Julian with a violent precision that no mere human could have controlled. Julian deftly blocked the blow and parried with several of his own.

Marduk dodged and blocked the blows, but he was a hairsbreadth slower than Julian. Julian swooped the staff behind Marduk's knees and sent him sprawling.

Ramiel let out an animalistic growl and charged Julian. The two men feinted and parried, staves knocking together with loud explosions of sound. Their struggles went on for several minutes, both men almost evenly matched. But Julian was patient and bided his time. He moved as if to bring the staff down on Ramiel's shoulder, then, at the last second, changed direction and hit the vampire across the stomach with a painful, audible *thwap*. Ramiel stumbled, still growling like an enraged animal.

The two men eyed each other then lowered their weapons. "Will I ever win against you, Julian?" Ramiel's voice echoed eerily in the practice room.

"I have trained more than you, Ramiel. That's all."

"No. You're too fast. Even for us." He nodded toward Marduk, who was resting against a far wall, watching. "We simply cannot compete."

"You are both formidable warriors. The best of the best. I trust no others with my life the way I entrust it to you both. I would fight beside no others as we three fight together. It doesn't matter who's faster, more skilled, more deadly, we are a team."

Ramiel smiled, revealing a small glint of fang. "How gallant of you."

"So did you find anything on your hunt tonight?" Marduk asked, abruptly changing the subject as he was wont to do.

For some reason Julian didn't want to mention Brandi to these two men, no matter that he trusted them implicitly. He wanted to keep his burgundy-haired vixen a secret, one solely for himself, just for a little while. "I found a bogle." It wasn't a lie.

"Damn black spirits," Marduk spat. "There are too many of them loose. We need to find the keys soon, before we are overrun."

"We shall find the keys," Julian assured them. "Until then...let's get the lead out, shall we?" He grinned. "Come on, the both of you, take me down. *If* you can," he goaded.

Laughing, Marduk picked up his staff once more and both he and Ramiel rushed Julian as one.

The fight lasted half an hour, with all three men sweating profusely in the last grueling minutes. But no matter that it lasted so long, neither Ramiel nor Marduk were able to take Julian down. And, quite simply, they never would. Among the three of them, despite the others' otherworldly talents, Julian was the greatest fighter. Which was good. Since he was, after all, their leader.

* * * * *

Once again, Brandi awoke to the sound of a fist pounding on her front door. She growled a curse and rolled out of the makeshift bed she'd fashioned on her couch. She stomped over to the door and opened it, unsurprised to see a uniformed man standing there with his fist poised in the air, ready to beat on the door once more.

"Deputy Little. What brings you here?" she asked, already knowing the answer.

"The sheriff wants you to come in with me."

"Am I being arrested?" she asked.

Brian Little blushed and offered her an apologetic smile. "No. He just wants to badger you a little, I think." He sighed heavily. "I'm sorry, Brandi. But you'll have to get dressed and come with me now."

"Shit," she spat, giving the deputy her back as she turned and went into the house, to her bedroom, to change into something more acceptable for daywear than her rumpled pajama shirt and shorts. She grabbed a well-worn pair of jeans and a t-shirt that had the words "Bite me" emblazoned on the front. She slammed the bedroom door closed and went about getting dressed.

Ten minutes later she settled into the back of the deputy's cruiser and stared blankly out the window. She didn't know what to expect once she was in the sheriff's clutches. Brandi was certain she wouldn't enjoy the experience one iota. She tried to get her mind prepared for the trial ahead, but her brain was a quagmire of discontent.

"So deputy, how are you enjoying our fair town?" She decided a little conversation might just calm her frayed nerves. She didn't know much about the deputy, except that his family was originally from Maryland and he took his status as lawman very seriously.

"I'm still loving it so far. Let me tell you, it's much more serene than D.C., that's for sure."

"Yeah, well, except for a child-stealing monster, I think this is a pretty cool place to be."

"Look, why don't you just let the matter go? The sheriff is going to catch the perpetrator—which isn't a mythical beast, I'm sure. All you're doing is making yourself look more and more unstable. Let it go. Let us do our job."

Brandi rolled her eyes and blew a stray lock of hair off her face. "I have proof. Several tapes of it, in fact. How do you explain that away, huh?"

"Ms. Carroll, you don't know how patient the sheriff has been with you up to this point. I've seen how distraught he gets when a family leaves town because of what you've shown them."

"Call me Brandi. And you didn't answer my question."

Deputy Little was silent for several minutes, lost in his own thoughts. "Well…I don't know how, but you must have faked the tapes."

Brandi was incredulous. "How in the hell would I do that? I have no formal training in the special effects field. The parents are always there when I call out the boogeyman—right there, with nothing but a door between us. They would know if I had faked the tape, deputy."

"Please call me Brian. And Brandi, I'm on your side. I know you've been under tremendous stress since your nephew was taken. You're allowed some eccentricities, that's for sure. And I think there's more going on here than we know, but I don't believe the culprit is a monster. I just can't swallow that pill, you know?"

"Why not?"

"Well for one, I just don't believe it. It's too fantastical. There are no such things as monsters."

"I wish I felt the same," she sighed. "I really do."

"Maybe you should, you know, talk to someone about all this."

"You mean go to a shrink. No way. I'm not crazy. There *is* a monster. Eventually the sheriff will realize that and then maybe, together, we can find a way to stop it."

"I doubt the sheriff will ever believe a monster is taking the children of Mt. Airy. I'm sorry, Brandi."

"It's okay, Brian. I'm used to it by now. Few people believe, until the monster stops at their house. Then you'd be surprised at who would swear by the beast's existence. You'd be very surprised."

"They're just grieving parents, nothing more," Brian said softly. "They're susceptible to any suggestion, even a paranormal one."

"I don't suggest; I *show* them what the monster looks like."

"Why are you doing this, Brandi? What can you hope to accomplish?" He glanced at her in his rearview mirror.

"I don't know." She slumped in the seat. "But one day I'll find a way to kill the monster and then I can go back to my regular life."

"I hope you can someday, Brandi. I really do."

"Me too," she sighed and, mute, looked out of the window as they drove to the station.

Chapter Seven

Sheriff Adams stepped into the tiny interrogation room where Brandi had been left waiting for the past two long hours. He sat in a chair opposite her, nothing but a little table between them, and he eyed her angrily. "I hear you've been making more movies."

Brandi sneered. "So? Is that a crime?"

"It could be, if I worded it just right in my paperwork."

"Don't threaten me, Sheriff. *Never* threaten me."

He sighed heavily and wiped a hand over his eyes. "I don't know what else to do with you. I told you to stop making tapes of the supposed monster. I told you to stop showing those tapes to distraught parents. Why didn't you stop?"

"The Bailys wanted me to show them. They asked me to come. I didn't volunteer."

"No, you never volunteer, do you? It's a good way to keep your nose clean. I can't arrest you for harassment if the family asked you to come, can I? Very smart of you."

"I gain nothing from showing these parents the truth. In fact, it nearly makes me sick every time I do it. Why would you think I would lie about this?" she cried.

"Brandi, I've known you for years. I never took you for a liar. But in the past three years, you've changed. You've practically become a recluse up there in your sister's house. You let people spread rumors about you until your reputation was in tatters. Why? I know you lost your nephew, but this is taking grief a bit too far. Just tell me why."

"Because of what is real. The monster is real. The children who go missing are real. Somehow I will find a way to destroy the monster and stop the nightmare. I can't accept anything less. In the meantime, I don't care what the town thinks of me, nor do I care what *you* think. I know I'm only showing these parents the truth—if they didn't want to know it, they would never contact me."

"I'm going to ask you one last time to put a stop to this. If you buck against me, in any way, I *will* have to arrest you."

"For what?" she snapped.

"Obstruction of justice, for one thing. We're looking for a kidnapper and all you're doing is making our job harder. Once you've shown your tapes to a family, they have practically nothing else to do with our investigation. They believe what you show them and ignore the very real threat out there."

"Please just watch my tapes. Maybe once you've seen them you'll believe too," she said through gritted teeth.

"I don't need to see your tapes. I won't let it be known around town that I've put any faith or credence in what you're doing." He twisted his lips with distaste. "No doubt they're fakes and I'm not even going to waste one red cent of our budget on forensics tests to prove that. There are no such things as monsters and your hysterics aren't doing anything but making you look like a fool."

Brandi nearly lost it. "They are not fakes. I'm not lying, dammit!"

"Don't interfere again. I'm warning you for the last time. We've already had a handful of people move because of your shenanigans. I don't want you scaring anyone else. Am I making myself clear?"

"Crystal," she gritted out, clenching her fists so tightly her nails broke the skin of her palms and the tiny wounds started to bleed.

"I'm letting you off easy, this is my last warning, but next time will be different. I will bust your little ass if you keep this up. All right?"

No, it wasn't all right. But Brandi nodded her assent anyway, wanting nothing more than to crawl back to her house and hide out for at least a week. She bit her lip until it too bled, to hold back all the words she wanted to say, and waited for what would come next.

"You can go home now. Try and get some sleep. You look like hell." The sheriff got up and left the room before Brandi could explode. She looked like hell because people like him kept interrupting what little sleep she'd been able to get! But she refrained from saying it aloud—something for which she was infinitely proud. She held her tongue and let the sheriff leave.

Deputy Little came into the room a few seconds later. "Ready to go?" he asked gently.

Brandi still couldn't trust herself to speak so, instead, she nodded and followed Brian out to his car, ignoring the stares and murmured words that dogged at her heels. She had her head down, looking only at the ground in front of her.

That was how she saw Julian's scary boots just a second before she ran into him.

Julian caught her before she could fall. His hand grabbed her upper arm—he seemed inclined to do that—and he steadied her.

"What are you doing here?" she spat to cover up her humiliation at being caught walking out of the police station with an armed escort.

"Coming after you," he said flatly, looking less than pleased to be there.

"Excuse me, Brandi, do you know this man?" Brian asked, appearing at a loss.

"Yeah, I know him."

"She'll be coming with me, deputy," Julian said commandingly.

"All right, then." Brian shrugged and left here there, without even asking her if she was willing to go with Julian. She wasn't. And it chafed that she had no control over it. It was ten miles to her house and she needed a ride.

She docilely followed Julian to his waiting motorcycle.

"I hate riding on that thing," she muttered under her breath.

Julian heard her words and rounded on her, eyes burning fiercely. "Lady, this *thing* is a *Hayabusa*. It's one of the fastest, most coveted bikes in the world."

"Well excuse me," she said, words heavy with sarcasm. "I don't like riding this *Himalaya*."

"*Hayabusa*," he spat.

"Yeah, that." She decided right then and there she enjoyed baiting Julian immensely.

"Get on," he commanded, swinging his own leg over the seat. He turned on the bike and it rumbled to life. Brandi reluctantly crawled onto the seat behind him and he revved the engine impatiently. The moment her arms came around his waist, they were off, at speeds Brandi didn't care to contemplate.

The wind bit at her exposed skin and she wished desperately for a helmet, but it didn't look like Julian even owned one. She could feel people watching them as they sped past and wondered what they thought of her sitting so closely, intimately, to a stranger as large and fearsome-looking as Julian.

She was sure to get a call from her sister about this—even though Gail had left the town, it didn't mean she wasn't all caught up on town gossip. People tended to stay in touch around Mt. Airy, no matter the distance. News of this was bound to hit her ears sooner or later.

After another wild ride down the dirt road, Julian brought the bike to a halt and dismounted. He helped her down, casually gallant, and followed her into the house.

"What happened?" he asked the moment the door was closed.

"It's none of your damn business," she said scathingly.

"It is now. What happened?"

"What do you mean 'it is now'?" she asked, walking to the kitchen. "I don't have to answer to you, so just back off. Or better yet, answer *my* question. How did you know where I was today?"

His lips twisted in a wry smile, sending her heartbeat soaring. "I came into town early. People talk around here. All I had to do was listen."

"Shit. Isn't that the truth," she said, putting two glasses on the table, filling them with milk.

"So what happened?" Julian reached for one of the glasses and drank half the milk in one gulp.

"You sound so concerned," she remarked sarcastically.

"I am. So what happened?" he asked again.

Brandi sighed. "The sheriff wants me to stop filming the monster. He thinks I'm inciting some sort of panic and interfering with his investigation. He had me brought in to the station this morning, hoping to scare me. It worked, the bastard." She took a large swig of her milk.

"Did he threaten you?" he asked menacingly.

Brandi never wanted to be on the receiving end of Julian's anger, that was for sure. "Sort of. Well…yeah, I guess he did."

Julian's face hardened.

"But he won't do anything," she hastened to add. "He's really too busy to worry much about me. Besides, I'm through filming the monster. I'll just have to settle for what I have here in the house to get further footage. I'll get the monster back here eventually."

"Why on earth would you want to call the monster to you?"

"So I can maybe find a way to kill it."

"How?"

"I don't know," she shrugged. "Something will come to me, I'm sure."

"Wait. Wait a minute." He set his glass down on the table with a great show of patience. "Are you saying that you wait for this thing? *Here*?"

"Yeah, in the back bedroom. It used to be my nephew's room. I sleep there now."

He gestured to the hall closet, just around the corner. "You've boarded up all the closets but one, the one in your bedroom?"

"Yeah."

"Are you mad, woman?" he thundered. "Do you have any idea of the danger you court?"

"That was some pretty way of saying I'm crazy."

"Quit joking around. This is not a laughing matter," he growled.

Brandi laughed, then immediately choked. Her vision grayed and she cried out, falling to the floor in a boneless heap.

Julian could only watch helplessly while Brandi had her vision. He knew it was a vision, for he too had them at times. But he could control them. They didn't lay him low as they did Brandi, not since he was a young boy centuries ago. He would have to teach her how to keep the visions at bay. Seconds ticked by and he easily lifted her up off the floor and carried her to the couch in the sitting room. He laid her down gently, sat on the floor next to her and waited for her to come back to herself.

He studied her face. It was delicate and elfin, completely feminine. He rather liked looking at it. She had sculpted brows, long, long lashes and skin that looked as if it were made from cream. Her nose was small and her lips were full and curvaceous. Her jaw kept her from looking too childish, giving her more of a stubborn look than anything.

Her body...her body made him hard just thinking about it. And looking at it as she lay there in a stupor made his loins positively ache. She had a full hourglass look that society frowned upon these days, but he loved a woman with some flesh on her. Her breasts were large and firm and he wondered what her nipples looked like. Would they be plump and juicy? Would they be dark or rosy? He intended to find out eventually. He'd known that the moment he'd clapped eyes on her.

Her hips were wide — proof that she could mother many fine babes should she choose to. Her legs were shapely and long, her feet tiny and adorable in her thong sandals. She was small; he was at least a foot taller than she. But he didn't mind. In fact, it made him feel more protective toward her than he might have otherwise, her smallness. He bent close and inhaled her scent. It made his head reel, it was such an exotic, erotic scent. He almost felt drunk on it.

The color of her hair mesmerized him. It wasn't quite red, it wasn't quite black, but somewhere in between. Burgundy. And the color was real; he could tell by the shade of her lashes and eyebrows. He toyed with a long lock of it, marveling at its silky texture. He wondered idly what the hair on her pussy looked like.

Minutes ticked by and Brandi remained motionless on the couch. He thought briefly of waking her up, of interrupting the vision, but he knew that it could end up hurting her so he let it go. Instead he rose and paced the length of the sitting room.

Curiosity got the better of him and he wandered to the back of the house, where Brandi's bedroom was located. He noted that her scent was most heavy here, where she slept. Or didn't sleep, as the case may be. He'd noticed the makeshift bed on the couch — it was apparent that she slept there, at least sometimes, where there were no open closets to bedevil her. No monsters to come for her as she dreamed. But still, her delicious perfume permeated the whole room, tickling his nose, making his pulse beat a wild staccato.

He noticed the video and computer equipment immediately. How could he not—the room was filled with wires and gadgets, techno-crap that he couldn't and wouldn't ever understand. He supposed he was showing his age, but he didn't trust electronic equipment at all. He marveled that Brandi could make any sense of the mess he saw.

The closet caught his attention. It was not, of course, boarded up as it should have been. He shook his head at Brandi's foolhardiness. One thing was for certain. She had courage in spades.

Good. She would need it in the days ahead.

He turned his back warily to the closet door, walked back to the living room and sat in a well-worn recliner, waiting for her to awaken.

She did. With a violent jerk and a gasp, she shot upright on the couch. Blood trickled from her nose, like a tiny crimson river. Julian reached into his pocket and brought out a handkerchief, handing it to her.

"Are you all right?" he asked.

She nodded unsteadily. "That was a bad one. The monster is going to strike again. Soon."

"I know," he said. "It seems the bogle is determined to rid your town of children."

"Why won't these visions stop?" she moaned, holding her head back and stemming the flow of blood with his crisp, white handkerchief. Well it was ruined now, she thought.

Brandi eyed him, wondering what was going on behind his witchy eyes. Did he think her truly mad now that she was claiming to have visions? If not for all she'd personally witnessed, she would have certainly questioned her own sanity. She couldn't help but feel self-conscious when he was around.

She noted that he had carried her to the couch—how could she not have?—and felt her cheeks burn with embarrassment. She was by no means a lightweight. She wondered how his back felt and almost laughed.

The bleeding had slowed to a trickle. Brandi folded his handkerchief and placed it in her lap. "I don't think I can get the stains out, but I'll try," she said apologetically.

"Don't worry. I have dozens more."

Brandi studied him, trying and failing not to eat him up with her eyes. He was just such a...male. Actually, he was maleness personified. She couldn't help but admire him. With his chiseled good looks and his powerfully muscular form, he nearly took her breath away. She shook her head to clear it of licentious thoughts. "Look, I don't mean to be rude or anything, but just what are you doing here? You don't know me. You have no reason to seek me out." She leaned forward with one eyebrow raised questioningly. "Are you a stalker?"

Julian let out a bark of laughter.

"Just throwing it out there as a possibility," she quipped, grinning and leaning back into the sofa.

"I assure you, I am not stalking you."

"Then what are you doing here?" she asked.

"I needed to talk to you about some things."

Brandi frowned. "What sorts of things?"

"How long have you had the visions?" he asked, changing the subject.

She took a big breath and sighed. "Ever since my nephew disappeared."

"I can teach you how to control them," he said after a beat.

"Oh yeah, I forgot. You're a paranormal investigator. I guess this must be pretty much routine for you now, huh?" she asked hopefully.

His lips turned up in a little smile. "Not like you're thinking. No. But I know a lot about visions. Trust me. I can help you to control yours, but it will take practice."

"I'd do practically anything to get a hold on these damn things."

Julian's eyes widened and filled with a carnal heat that made her squirm in her seat. "I don't mean *that*. I said *practically* anything."

He laughed, then stopped abruptly, looking as if he had surprised himself with the sound.

"You don't laugh much, do you Julian?" she noted.

"We were talking about you," he said, pointedly ignoring her question. "But I can show you some things you could practice when I leave. Now, how much do you know about your family's history?"

The question caught her off guard. "Actually, I'm not sure I know enough. My dad's heritage comes from Scotland. I think maybe my mom's is from England."

"Your family hasn't ever had a genealogist make a record of your family tree?"

"Yeah, like before I was born," she answered, shrugging. "Where are you going with these questions?"

"I did some research last night. After seeing you call to the bogle, I knew there was something special about you. Not everyone has the power to perform such a feat. So I did a little rooting around and I think I know why you're able to do what you do."

"Why?" she urged.

"Several generations back, you had a nobleman in your family. He was able, with his power and position, to send his youngest son to squire with the Knights Templar. The boy grew up to become a Knight himself, and a magnificent warrior he was too. He married and had children before dying on the battlefield. His blood runs in your veins. It is a powerful heritage, even now, hundreds of years later. You have gained much from this long-dead ancestor. It is how you were able to fight the bogle. It is why, in this time of danger, you are having visions that foretell of even greater danger."

"The Knights Templar? Get out of here. I thought they were just a myth."

"No. They are very much real. Though in the fourteenth century many of them were hunted down, tortured and put to death, they were a major driving force in history. For hundreds of years they were the wealthiest, most powerful of men. They were thought to have sacred knowledge, sacred arts. Magic. No one but the Pope had power over them."

"And I descend from one of these Knights?"

"Yes. And through this bloodline, you have inherited many abilities. I believe I can help you to discover them, if you like."

"If this heritage is responsible for my brushes with the bogle, then I don't want to have anything to do with it."

"If you change your mind, my offer will stand. You should give it consideration before you dismiss it out of hand. There is much I could teach you."

"But how do you know so much?"

"Because I...because I also have an ancestor who was a Templar Knight. I have inherited these same abilities," he answered hesitantly. "I've learned how to use them. You can too, though it may take time."

Brandi sensed that there was more to his story, but she held her tongue. "I can't believe what you're saying. I don't believe in hocus-pocus."

"How do you explain away your visions, then?"

Brandi let out a pent-up breath. "I can't. But that doesn't really bother me," she hastened to add. "I've gotten used to them. They're just a quirk, that's all. Like a tic that I can't get rid of."

"What about your ability to call the bogle?" he asked.

"Until you came along, I wasn't sure that was what I was doing. I just assumed that the bogle remained in the same home for a few days, just to make sure it didn't have any more prey. I thought I was just there to record its visitation."

"You were calling to it."

"Then why can't I get him to come through *my* bedroom closet?" she demanded to know.

"I think perhaps because that way is sealed against it. Somehow, without your meaning to, you have prevented the bogle from revisiting this place despite your best efforts, placed wards to hold him at bay."

"But I *want* him to come! Why would I seal the way?" she cried.

"You didn't mean to, that's obvious. Again, it's all to do with your heritage. A heritage I can help you to better understand and appreciate, if you would only let me. Perhaps we can even find a way to open your door to the bogle…but I don't suggest you try it."

"This is insane. I can't believe I'm even listening to this."

"So you can believe in the boogeyman and in your visions, but you have a problem with knowing you've a great legacy to aid you should you choose to use it?"

"Shut up." She frowned fiercely. "I just need time to adjust, that's all."

He moved to sit next to her on the couch. She moved over to give him room, but he still seemed to swallow up the space with his large body. "I need you to think about something for me," he said softly.

"What," she asked suspiciously.

"Was there anything unusual that happened in the days leading up to your nephew's disappearance?"

Brandi thought for a long moment then shook her head. "I can't think of anything."

"Well try to, in the next few days. It could be anything, small or large, just try to see if you remember something that might have been different. Anything at all."

"I will," she nodded.

The warmth of his thigh, pressed against hers, made her heart jump and beat wildly. Julian seemed to know what she was feeling. He leaned close, his breath smelling of sweet cinnamon, and cupped his hand around her neck. The domineering hold he had on her didn't scare her, not at all, instead it made her nipples hard and her mouth burn for his kiss. His other hand went around her back and steadied her, pulling her even closer to him.

He tilted her head back, just so, and pressed his lips to hers. All coherent thought fled and she was like putty in his arms. She sighed, lips parting, and he caught her breath with his mouth before plundering her depths with his tongue. The flavor of him was wild and masculine. His tongue slid alongside hers, deep and hot. He bit her full bottom lip, as if he would eat her up, and laved the small bite with his tongue.

Brandi was lost. She had been the first moment he'd laid his hands upon her at the Bailys', and what's more, she'd known it then. Her body quivered and he pulled her even closer into his embrace. His big hand was splayed over her back, fingers gently massaging her. He slanted his lips over hers and crushed her against his chest. Her nipples were diamond hard and so sensitive, pressed firmly against his big, muscular chest.

The hand around her throat wandered to the nape of her neck, where he tangled his fingers in her hair. He let out a sound, much like a growl, and she swallowed it. Her lips were swelling underneath his, softening. She let him take all of her, let her worries and her troubles go. She was lost in the moment as she never had been before with but a mere kiss.

A mere kiss? Lord but this was so much more than that. It made her head spin to even contemplate the repercussions of this sudden and fierce attraction.

Julian pulled back and licked her lips erotically. She moaned and melted farther against him. His hand moved down her back and cupped her buttocks so that she gasped. She grew wet against her panties, her sex aching, empty and bereft.

He could have taken her in that moment. She wouldn't have stopped him. But instead he pulled away and took her hands in his. He brought them up and softly kissed the knuckles on each hand. "Before this can go any further, I would like to explain a few things to you." His voice was ragged and slightly breathless.

"What?" Her voice was husky, alien to her ears.

"I don't know…" He faltered, seeming at a loss for further words. "It may not be the right time. If you're having trouble with learning the truth about yourself, you'll definitely have trouble with this."

Brandi didn't care what he had to say. She wanted more of his delicious kiss. She jumped into his lap and wrapped her legs around him. She put her hand in his hair and pulled him toward her. She licked his lips as he had licked hers, his tongue venturing out and touching hers once more. She sighed wantonly. Opening her mouth wide to receive the thrust of his tongue, she couldn't help but moan and thrust hers into his mouth in return.

Julian kissed his way over to her jawline, licking her there. His mouth wandered down over her throat, where he sucked her skin between his teeth. Brandi cried out at the love bite, but not in pain. She rubbed herself against him, noting how incredibly large and hard he was. Hell, he was large all over, and the enormous size of the cock held captive behind his tight jeans shouldn't have surprised her. But it did nonetheless.

She heard him breathing in her scent as his face was pressed to her throat. Felt his tongue lave her skin. Felt his hands biting into her thighs, holding her tight against him. "Oh, Julian," she moaned breathlessly. His hands tightened on her further.

"We have to stop," he said gruffly against her flesh, his accent heavy and thick, but his hold on her didn't let up despite his words.

Brandi could only whimper in response.

His hands tightened on her once more then, reluctantly, let her go. He pushed her off his lap inelegantly and rose, running a hand through his hair so that long strands escaped the tie at his nape.

They were both silent as their breathing slowed, neither meeting the other's gaze.

"I'm sorry," she said unsteadily. "I don't know why I did that. You're practically a stranger. I'm not usually like this."

"Don't apologize," he said raggedly. "Don't you dare."

"Your hair is mussed," she pointed out, smiling shakily.

Julian grinned, looking positively delectable. "So is yours." He began backing away toward the front door. "I have to go. But there is still much I wish you to know. Can I pick you up in the morning?"

"Will you be riding your bike?"

He rolled his eyes. "Yes."

She thought for a moment the sighed in resignation. If she had to endure a motorcycle ride to be with him then so be it. She was having too much fun to back out now. "All right. In the morning. Make it late so I can get a little sleep in, though."

"I'll drop by at about eleven. How's that?"

Brandi couldn't believe, after that wild explosion of passion between them, that they were speaking so casually to one another. "That sounds great," she murmured.

Without a word of goodbye, he turned and left. She heard the rumble of his bike as he drove away and decided she needed to take a very long, very cold shower.

She could only hope that he felt the same.

Chapter Eight

Julian sped through the streets as if he owned them. He drove aimlessly, taking little-traveled back roads, flying by chicken farms and pastures without so much as a glance at the beautiful, rolling countryside. His thoughts weren't on the wild ride between his legs, but on the ride he could have given Brandi between hers.

He could have had her, he knew. He could have possessed her hot, tempting little body as she had possessed his thoughts ever since the moment they met. But he couldn't. Not with so many secrets left between them. He had a feeling Brandi would be more than just a romp between the sheets. She was so sultry, so passionate. She was meant for permanent loving, not some sticky fumbling on her living room couch. There must be no secrets between them. Nothing to get in the way of their future together, should it come to that.

God but his cock was so hard it hurt.

His whole body was hard with need. It was a testament to his lack of control that he actually thought about going back and taking what she had offered so innocently to him in her wild passion. But he merely sped up, as if to escape the temptation that lay behind him, and roared down the endless, winding country road.

The taste of her was still abloom on his tongue. His lips tingled with the memory of her softer ones pressed tight against them. She had felt so right in his arms it had scared him a little. He who was afraid of nothing was laid low by a tiny woman with a mouth like a siren. It was laughable, only he didn't feel like laughing at all.

He could almost smell her on his skin. It was driving him mad.

With an animalistic growl, he turned his bike around, peeling rubber and headed in the direction he felt sure the interstate lay. He would go back to Atlanta for the night, and prepare himself for what he knew must come next. He'd need to use his fist to clear his mind of his wanton thoughts, but he was no stranger to such relief. But next time, he vowed, he'd come not in his hand but deep inside Brandi's very sexy body.

* * * * *

The next morning Brandi opened the door and stepped out on her porch, and was surprised to see that Julian had actually brought a car instead of his motorcycle. "Be still my heart," she muttered blithely.

Julian came around to the passenger's side of the bright red sports car and opened the door for her. He was wearing his voluminous black coat, and her heart tripped. He was so gorgeous it made her mouth dry with yearning. She pushed her giddy response to him away and slid into the car, noting the soft, plush leather interior, and breathed deep of Julian's scent, which still lingered inside the little car. "Where are we going?" she asked as he took the driver's seat.

"Atlanta."

Brandi's eyes widened. "Why Atlanta? I hate that friggin' place."

"Because that's where we need to go," he said flatly.

She snorted. "Fine, be that way." She leaned closer to him and grinned devilishly. "Did you think of me last night?"

He gritted his teeth and gripped his hand on the wheel, practically flying down the dirt road. "Stop playing around."

With a sigh, she settled back in her seat, watching the road go by. It would be at least an hour's trip to Atlanta, depending on what part of the great city he was headed for. She hoped they weren't going downtown—that place gave her the heebie jeebies. She much preferred her quiet, close-knit town to the big city.

It was so silent in the car that Brandi soon found herself dozing. She leaned her seat back and put her arm over her eyes. Sleep was just beyond her reach—she hadn't slept but a few hours the night before after all—and it felt good. She realized with a small jolt that she felt totally safe with Julian, even though she barely knew him. It was easy for her to relax in his presence. She hadn't felt anything even close to this feeling since before Nick disappeared.

How, in so short a time, had she become so attached to this man? So trusting of him? She didn't know, but the attraction between them was palpable now and the sexual tension could have been cut with a knife. There was something about this man that reached into all the dark corners of her life, sweeping away her worries and fears. It scared her a little, the sheer power of it. She knew Julian was capable of violence. Danger fairly radiated off him in waves. But still, she wanted him.

She closed her eyes and went to sleep, lulled by the murmur of the car's powerful engine and by Julian's presence at her side.

When she awoke, they were pulling into a parking space outside a large brick building. She frowned and looked around. The building was very plain, with no markings at all. It was surrounded on three sides by dense, thick woodland. The only entrance was through a massive wrought iron gate. Brandi couldn't be sure, but she thought this place was probably a little off the beaten path. It had an air of secrecy about it that had her wondering what might happen next.

Julian got out of the car and walked around to open her door. Brandi opened it hurriedly, before he could reach for the handle, and stepped out, ignoring his outstretched hand. She supposed she was stubborn that way.

"What is this place?" she asked.

"I guess you could call it my office," he answered.

"Why are we here?"

"I want you to meet some people."

"Who?"

"Wait and see." He reached into his pocket and pulled out a small, shiny, black leather wallet. He took a card out and swiped it through the electronic lock beside the building's front door. There was a *click*, and the door automatically opened before them. He motioned her forward and followed, the door closing with an audible *snick* of the lock sliding home behind them.

He led her into a great, wide room with a shining marble floor. There was a symbol of a pyramid with an eye floating above its point inlaid into the marble in the center of the room. Julian took her arm and led her to stand in the very center of that symbol. They stood there for a couple of seconds.

"What—" She broke off with a gasp as the floor beneath their feet started to lower, like an elevator with no walls. He brought her closer against him, so that her body was pressed against his from shoulder to knee. The floor sank to a second, underground chamber, where Julian took her hand and led her off the platform.

He led her from the great room and took her down many long, winding hallways. Brandi became completely disoriented, knowing she'd have to rely solely on Julian to get her out of there. The compound was massive, on such a large scale that she couldn't begin to guess where they were in relation to its entrance, left far behind them. She was hopelessly lost. In more ways than one.

At last, they stopped in front of a large, ornately carved wooden door at the end of one long, twisting corridor. Julian knocked and someone within told him to enter. They stepped into the room together, the door closing shut behind them, and Brandi saw a white-haired man behind a desk, watching them.

"My lord, I'd like you to meet Brandi Carroll," Julian said formally. "She is a descendant of the Order. I've brought her here today to…reveal some truths. Truths which I think she may have trouble believing from me, but from you I think she'll listen."

Brandi snorted, growing suddenly irritated with the two men for speaking to each other as if she wasn't even there.

"Are you sure this is wise?" the white-haired man asked after a long pause, during which he studied her thoroughly with his pale gray eyes.

"I believe so. She has been hunting a bogle that has overrun her town and she has been having visions, painful ones. I think she might bloom fully if we treat her with great care. I believe it's imperative that she learns more about herself, and us."

The man's eyes widened. "Are you certain this is what you want?"

"It is," Julian answered.

"She doesn't look like she'll be willing to listen."

"Yes, well." Julian cleared his throat. "I sort of surprised her with the trip here."

Brandi waved at them. "Hey, I'm still here, remember? I can hear everything you're saying."

Julian sighed. "She is very stubborn."

"I can see that." The man's eyes twinkled. "Very well, Brandi Carroll, please have a seat." He motioned to two comfy-looking chairs in front of his desk. "My name is Gregori. I pretty much run the business side of what we do here. Julian usually does the legwork, for which I am infinitely grateful," he chuckled. "So. What do you know of your heritage, my dear?" he asked without hesitating.

She briefly thought of ignoring his question, but something about the man made her want to find favor with him. She took her seat, Julian taking the other beside her.

"Only what Julian has told me, and what little I remember from my parents," she answered at last.

"Do you know anything about the Knights Templar?" Gregori asked gently, smiling benevolently.

Brandi shook her head. She couldn't help but begin to like this man. There was just something so completely charming about him.

"There is much myth about the Knights. Much speculation. But we here know the truth behind the mystery. For we are all Knights ourselves."

"Don't you mean you're *descendents* of the Knights?"

Gregori smiled. "No. We *are* Knights. Every one of us here."

"How many more of you are there?"

"About a dozen or so," Julian answered.

"I thought the Knights Templar were disbanded in the Middle Ages. That's what Julian said."

"In the fourteenth century, yes. They were captured and tortured, some put to death, others banished to lifelong imprisonment. But a few of us escaped the carnage. We've hidden for centuries but we have never left our duties behind."

"What are those duties?" she asked, curious.

"To protect the innocent. To keep evil from overrunning the world. To preserve history, even as we make it."

"I don't see what that has to do with me." She frowned.

"You have the blood of heroes running through you veins. Surely you've had instances where you thought of the phone and it rang. When you knew you were about to have a surprise visitor. You have an undeniable urge to protect the innocent. You feel responsible for their welfare, stranger or no. Am I right?"

Brandi thought for a moment and realized that Gregori was right. "So what does it mean?"

"It means that you have the same power your ancestors possessed. It merely needs to be carefully awakened. With the proper training, you could achieve that."

"This all seems a little farfetched, you know?" She couldn't help feeling skeptical.

Gregori nodded. "Shall I tell her more, Julian? Be sure you wish to travel down this road."

Julian sighed. "Tell her everything."

"My dear, we here are more than just guardians of the innocent. So much more. We have powers that mere mortals could never understand. We have arcane knowledge that many would kill to know."

"You're talking about magic?" She scoffed, then caught herself—why not magic? She'd discovered stranger things existed in this topsy-turvy world.

Gregori smiled. "A demonstration then. Julian, will you do the honors?"

Julian nodded and stood up. He rolled his head around on his shoulders, loosening up his muscles. He stilled, icy blue eyes burning with white-hot fire. He muttered something under his breath, something Brandi couldn't hear or understand. The forefinger of his right hand traced little circles in the air. A flash of light burst in the room and when it dimmed, there was a glowing golden halo surrounding Julian's body.

"W-what's that?" she asked, incredulous, jumping up from her seat in shock.

"This is merely a protection spell. I could do other, more impressive tricks, but the room isn't big enough for that," Julian said calmly.

"Why are you showing me this?" she cried.

"Because you need to know. Because there are greater things at work here and you're a part of that. You need to understand how powerful you can be. With the proper guidance," Julian answered, the halo still burning bright around him.

"I can't believe this," she muttered, putting her hand to her head to wipe away at sudden droplets of sweat.

Gregori turned to Julian. "I don't understand why you brought her here. You could have shown her this trick without my aid."

The glow around Julian's body dissipated then disappeared completely. "I brought her because I had to. There was no alternative. She needs to know as much about us as possible, for she," Julian took a big breath before letting it out, "is the seventh key."

Chapter Nine

Gregori looked startled. "My God. Are you certain of this?"

"Yes, my lord," Julian nodded. "At first I was disbelieving as well. But it cannot be denied. She *is* the seventh key."

"But how can this be?"

"I don't know. But I believe the truth will be revealed with time," Julian answered.

Gregori leaned back in his seat and pressed his fingers to the corners of his eyes. "All the other keys were inanimate objects, objects I could understand the use of. What does this mean, that she is the seventh and final key?"

"It means she must join us in the quest for the sixth key. It means that she must be there when we open the gate."

"What are you talking about?" Brandi asked, growing more and more nervous with each uttered word.

Julian took the seat next to her once more and turned to face her. "We are looking for the fabled Seven Keys of Solomon, keys that will unlock the gate to the netherworld."

Brandi's eyes bulged. "Why on earth would you want to do something like that?" she demanded loudly.

A look of infinite patience had settled over Julian's features. "When we open the gate, all the monsters of this world will be called back to it, for hell wants its minions. We'll force them back into the gate and use the keys to seal it shut behind them. Your monster, your bogle," he nodded, "it will be called back to the gate and sealed in with the rest of the dark creatures who've escaped the gates over the centuries."

"I don't believe this. I can't." Brandi shook her head emphatically. "Gates to hell and magic keys, I'm sorry but I just can't believe in them."

"You will," Julian promised softly, ominously.

Gregori cleared his throat. "If she is indeed the seventh key, then we must protect her at all costs."

"My feelings exactly," Julian agreed. "I was going to take Marduk and Ramiel with me to guard her, as we continue to look for the sixth key, if that is acceptable to you, my lord."

"Very wise of you," Gregori praised. "Shall I call them to come and meet her?"

Julian nodded. "Actually, have them come to my quarters, if you please. There are a few things I must get before we go. It may be a while before I return."

Gregori nodded. "As you wish. Good luck to you, my friend."

Julian rose and, taking Brandi's hand, he pulled her up from her seat.

"Do not be afraid, my dear," Gregori said. "Julian is my best man. He will not let any harm befall you."

Brandi swallowed hard and followed Julian out the door. He still held her hand captive in his, swallowing it up. He led her down corridor after winding corridor, completely disorienting her.

"How do you know I'm this key of yours?" she couldn't help asking.

Without slowing, Julian answered, "Because I felt it, the first moment I saw you. I just took the time I needed to be certain before I told you."

"Is that why you kissed me? To be certain?" she asked with a sudden, burning ire.

Julian stopped and she nearly tripped over her feet. His icy blue eyes burned with an inner fire that threatened to melt her as he met her gaze. "I kissed you because you're too fucking sexy for your own good," he said gruffly.

"Oh," she said, nonplussed.

He turned and continued down the hallway. Neither of them spoke. After much walking—the underground complex was truly, unbelievably enormous—they came at last to a door, which Julian opened with a bright brass key. "This is where I live when I'm away from home," he said, pushing the door wider for her to enter.

"And where do you call home?" she asked quizzically.

"Valdosta. It's a long drive between here and there, which is why I sometimes sleep here."

More than a little curious to see his home away from home, Brandi entered and looked around. It was dark until Julian pulled out a match and lit some antique-looking sconces on the wall. What she saw then, as the room lit with the dim light of the torches, was breathtaking. Rich, dark colors graced the room, which she assumed to be the sitting or living room. Reds and golds and blacks were everywhere. Textures of every type were in abundance. Plush pillows were strewn here and there as accents. It looked like a sultan's den.

She noted almost at once that there were no electrical appliances.

"I won't be but a minute," he said. "Have a seat and make yourself comfortable," he offered.

Brandi went to the big, red velvet couch and sat, breathing deep of the Nag Champa fragrance that permeated the room. The cushions of the couch swallowed her up with marshmallow softness and she leaned back wearily, trying to clear her befuddled thoughts.

There came a knock at the door. "Would you get that, please?" Julian called out from his bedroom, situated, she guessed, the very back of the apartment.

Brandi rose and opened the door, completely unprepared for what she would see on the other side.

A tall, blond man with bright amber eyes regarded her silently, as if he too were surprised to see her. He was muscular, though not half so much as Julian, and very tall. His lips were the most beautiful she'd ever seen on a man, lush and curvaceous. He had bronze-colored skin and she wondered idly what nationality he was. His hair was long, touching his shoulders, and wild with curls. His face was almost too pretty. He was beautiful, there was no other word for it.

He cleared his throat and Brandi realized she'd been staring.

"Uh, sorry." She laughed nervously. "I'm Brandi. Julian is in the back," she said, letting the man enter.

The man raised an eyebrow, studying her from head to toe. He nodded then, as if he'd come to a decision, and moved toward the bedroom.

Moments later, another knock shocked Brandi out of her stupor and she went to answer the door one more time. This time she was a little more prepared, but still not enough. She opened the door and found herself staring into the blackest eyes she'd ever seen.

This man was a little taller than the first, but not by too much. He was shorter than Julian, but much taller than herself. His skin was pale as cream, and his black hair and black eyes were in stark contrast to his coloring. Something about him — she couldn't put her finger on it — made her a little nervous. He was a predator. She could see it in his strange eyes.

He stepped in without a word of welcome and towered over her. She was so close to him she could have leaned forward and kissed his chest.

For some strange, alien reason, she had a powerful urge to do just that.

The man put his finger on her cheek and trailed it down to her throat. Brandi felt her head falling back before she could gather the wits to stop it. The man bent closer, dipping his head down to her. He drew in a long, deep breath and Brandi realized he was sniffing her. The heat of his tongue darted out and licked her flesh delicately. Brandi grew dizzy and began to sag helplessly against him.

"Stop it, Ramiel," Julian growled menacingly from behind her.

The man rose and shot her a cocksure grin. "She doesn't have your scent on her," he said quietly, his voice so melodious that Brandi would have sworn she could hear bells ringing in it.

"Regardless, she is off limits," Julian said insistently.

"As you wish," the man, Ramiel, said and backed away from her, releasing her from whatever spell he'd cast over her. Brandi gasped and stumbled backward, suddenly wanting as much distance between her and Ramiel as possible.

"Brandi, these are my friends, Marduk and Ramiel." Each man nodded to her in turn, though there was still that dark, knowing glance on Ramiel's face. "They will be helping me to protect you."

Brandi's eyes widened and she shivered despite herself. "I don't need protection," she argued.

Julian ignored her. "I need the two of you to accompany me to Mt. Airy," he said to his colleagues. "We must keep Brandi safe and secure at all costs."

"Why?" Marduk asked, eyeing her warily.

"Because she is the seventh key."

Both men's eyes widened, though Ramiel hid it better than Marduk. "A human? I don't understand. Until now the keys have all been inanimate objects," Marduk pointed out.

"I know," Julian said. "It surprised me too."

"What of the sixth key?" Ramiel asked softly. Brandi thought he kept his voice quiet to downplay the beauty of it. "Have you made any progress in recovering it?"

Julian was silent for a long moment, thinking. "I'm not sure yet. I didn't expect to find the seventh key so quickly. I admit, I've been so drawn to Brandi that I haven't given it my full attention."

Brandi blushed to the roots of her hair upon hearing this.

"But that will change once you join us," Julian continued, ignoring her. "I'll be able to focus on other matters, knowing that she is safe in her home with you two."

"Hey, wait a minute. No one's even asked me if they can stay with me yet," she protested. "What if I don't want two strangers in my house, huh?"

"Tough," Julian said, unapologetic. "You'll just have to deal with it."

Brandi was dumbstruck. She couldn't even begin to think how to respond to his highhanded words.

Julian looked at her and chuckled. "For once you're at a loss for words," he teased. "I knew it would happen one day."

Brandi gasped, frowned and shot him a bird.

He merely laughed and went about getting some pieces of luggage. "Marduk, Ramiel, I suggest you pack a few bags."

"Whoa, wait a minute! Just how long do you plan on staying with me?" she cried.

Julian's gaze met hers unwaveringly. "As long as it takes."

"No. *No.* I have a life—" she started.

"You have a fragmented life at best, Brandi, and you know it," he said ruthlessly. "Don't you want to find a way to fix that once and for all?"

Brandi bit her lip and tried to ignore the pain of his words. "How will this fix things?"

"Look, either you're with us or against us. By working with us, you can save the world from dark creatures like your bogle. By working against us, you'll force us to take drastic measures, practically keeping you prisoner inside your own house."

"You wouldn't dare," she gasped.

"Try me," Julian said flatly, glaring at her.

"I can't believe you're saying this to me," she gasped. "How dare you try to take over my life! It may be fragmented, as you say, but it *is* mine. Not yours! I think I should have some say in who stays with me in my own house."

Ramiel hissed and grabbed her shoulder. "Julian has made his decision and you will abide by it," he said through sharp, gritted teeth.

Brandi caught a glimpse of fangs and started. She looked up into Ramiel's now red, glowing eyes and she shrieked. "Holy hell!" She tried to wrest her shoulder free of his grasp but he was so strong. She would wear his bruises as proof of that.

"Cease and desist, Ramiel," Julian warned him.

The ebony-haired man immediately released her, red eyes fading back into black.

"What the fuck are you?" she said breathlessly, taking several steps back away from Ramiel. "How can your eyes possibly do that?"

"Calm down, Brandi," Julian said soothingly. "He's a nosferatu."

Brandi laughed, noting how close to hysteria it sounded. "Nosferatu? Are you on crack? There's no such thing!"

Ramiel smiled, revealing a very impressive, very wicked-looking set of fangs. "You're wrong."

She gasped and put even more distance between them, nearly tripping over Marduk in the process. He steadied her gently and she was grateful, else she might have fallen.

"B-but it's daylight. Aren't you supposed to be sleeping in your c-coffin?" she stammered weakly.

Ramiel's smile disappeared. "Propaganda. We vampires can and do walk about by day. Our powers are weakened in the sun, it's true, but that is all. We do not burn, we do not die. Such things are myths, nothing more."

"Oh my god, I can't believe I'm having this conversation," she wailed. "Are there any other potentially fatal things I need to know about, besides Mr. Fang-Face here?"

"You're in no danger," Julian said patiently. "Is she, Ramiel?"

Ramiel merely smiled. The elementally dangerous look on his face did nothing to placate her.

Brandi closed her eyes. "This is too much."

"Then you're really going to hate *this*," Marduk told her. "I'm a revenant."

"A what?" She frowned.

"A revenant. I am the returned dead. Over two thousand years ago I was sacrificed, then resurrected back to life."

"What does that mean?"

"It means I cannot die. Not by conventional means anyway. It means I have heightened strength, agility and killer instincts. But don't worry," he winked rakishly at her, "you'll be safe with me."

"Oh hell." Brandi wandered over to the couch and sat down heavily. "How can all this be possible? Secret societies, paranormal creatures—my god, a *vampire!*" She pointed accusingly at Ramiel. "It's just too much."

"There's more," Julian said softly, gently, going to one knee on the floor beside her.

Brandi moaned and squeezed her eyes shut.

"When Gregori said we are Templar Knights, he wasn't jesting. You see, we are *original* Knights, Gregori and I." He paused and took a breath. "I myself am from the thirteenth century."

Brandi cried out and put her hands over her ears. Julian gently pulled her hands away and held them in his. "It's true. I am over seven hundred years old. And I am immortal."

Brandi squeezed her eyes shut so tight she saw stars.

Chapter Ten

Later that afternoon Brandi sat quietly in the passenger's seat of Julian's car. Her brain was a mess of thoughts, none of them making much sense. Ramiel and Marduk followed behind them in an SUV. Julian was quiet, seemingly lost in his thoughts. The drive to her house was over an hour, and they'd already covered half the distance without saying a single word to each other.

At last, Brandi could stand it no longer. "How can you be immortal?" she asked weakly.

"I have drunk from the cup of life."

"The what?"

"The Holy Grail," he said patiently.

Her head reeled. "Are you saying that's real too?"

"True as blue," he answered, one corner of his mouth lifting in a grin.

"And Gregori has drunk from it?" When Julian nodded she went on. "What about Marduk and Ramiel?"

"They were made immortal by other means. Marduk was made immortal by the priests who resurrected him in Babylon over two thousand years ago. And Ramiel was made a vampire in the, uh, eighteenth century I believe. He won't say how, but I think a woman was involved."

"I can't believe all this is real. I feel like Alice."

"Lost down the rabbit hole." Julian smiled, the look softening his angular face. "There are many mysteries in this world. Many creatures, both good and evil. Why should you be so surprised at this? You've seen for yourself that there are extraordinary things at work in the world."

"I don't know. I just never expected all this." She waved her hands about. "I admit, I'm at a loss here."

"You'll adapt before you know it," Julian assured her.

"And what about this key thing? How can I be a key?"

"That's what we're going to find out."

"How do you know I'm this key?" she asked.

"I can feel it. I sense it."

"And you trust those senses?"

"I do," he answered. "They have never led me astray before."

"Good grief, this is unbelievable. I don't want to have a part in opening some gate to hell," she said unevenly. "It's crazy to even think of such a thing."

"But it is very real, nevertheless. You have the power to change the world. Aren't you eager to see it done?"

She thought for a long moment. "If it means getting rid of this monster, then I suppose I do want to see it done. Sooner rather than later, so I don't lose my nerve, you know?"

He nodded his understanding. "I feel much the same."

"But you must have bucket loads of courage, being immortal." She nearly choked on the words.

"We all have our doubts and our fears. I am no different from you in that regard."

"But why do I need to be guarded? I've made it all right so far."

"Because we can't let anything happen to you. If we lost you, we would lose our battle and our quest would be over. The world itself is at stake. Don't you think that deserves some special attention?"

She twisted her lips. "But I don't trust them—your friends. Especially Ramiel."

"He won't hurt you. He's just...well, frankly, he's a predator. He can't help his nature. But now that he knows how things stand, he won't bother you again. And Marduk is probably the most trustworthy man I've ever met. Nothing means more to him than honor. He would fight to the death to protect you."

"Except that he can't die," she pointed out.

Julian surprised her by shaking his head. "Though Marduk is immortal, he can be killed. Usually the severing of the head or the spinal column will do it. The same is true of Ramiel."

"What about you?"

He turned to glance at her, blue eyes bright. "I cannot die. The Grail's power is absolute."

Brandi shivered. "Bogles, vampires, revenants, gates to hell…I'd say I've had a full day, wouldn't you?" Sarcasm fairly dripped from her words.

Julian chuckled, the sound warming her insides despite her intentions not to let it do so. "You could say that."

"So what's to be done about this last key? I don't suppose you can open the gate without it?"

"No, we can't."

"Do you have any idea where it might be?" she asked, more than a little curious.

"Not yet," he answered. "And it may take some time before I find it. Finding you was accidental—I was on the trail of the sixth key, or so I'd thought. It usually takes me weeks or even months to pinpoint a key. But soon, with luck, I'll know more."

"Do you know what the key is? Is it another human?"

He glanced at her. "No. It's the Hope diamond."

Brandi felt her eyes go wide. "*The* Hope diamond? Are you sure?"

"Absolutely."

"Then you know where it is—it's at the Smithsonian," she said, pointing out the obvious.

Julian surprised her once more by shaking his head. "We've already gone there—the diamond that's currently on display is a fake. We think someone must have stolen the original."

"Oh...wow. That sucks."

"Yes. So you see our dilemma. It could be anywhere. It may take some time before I know where to search for it."

Brandi was silent for a long time, mind racing. "I'm not sure I want to bring this up, but you know how you told me I probably sealed the closet in my bedroom without realizing it?"

"Yes."

"Well, a few nights ago I was sitting there waiting for the bogle, when a man came through the door. He had a mask on so I didn't see his face, and he ran before I had a chance to corner him. How did he come through if the way was sealed shut? And how could he even get that far if he was just a human?"

Now Julian's eyes went wide with surprise. "Why didn't you tell me this sooner?" he exclaimed.

"So many stranger things have happened since that I just forgot," she said, half-apologetic. "I had the cameras rolling but they only recorded static from the time the man appeared until he'd run from the room," she rushed to tell him. "You can see it if you'd like. Not that it'll do you any good."

Julian frowned. "I'll have to think about this new development," he said. "It's most unexpected. In the meantime, if anything like this happens again, tell me immediately, understood?"

"God you're highhanded, aren't you?" She snorted. "But yeah, I'll tell you if I see anything else strange."

"Good." Julian leaned forward and turned on the stereo. For the rest of the trip they listened to a Hooverphonic CD. One thing was for certain, thought Brandi. Julian had excellent taste in music.

When they at last pulled into Brandi's driveway, she was none too pleased to note the deputy's car parked at her house.

"Shit," she mumbled, getting out of the car. "Just what I need."

Deputy Little came walking around the corner of the house. Brandi didn't like to think he may have been snooping on her property, but the thought was prevalent in her mind all the same. "What brings you here today, deputy?" she asked by way of greeting, with a lightheartedness she didn't feel.

"Brandi, I'm so glad I caught you. The sheriff wants to see you right away."

Brandi frowned. "Why, what's happened?"

The deputy flushed. "I'm not sure. I just know I'm supposed to take you down to the station."

Julian came up behind her and put a hand on her shoulder. For some reason that small gesture made a world of difference. She immediately relaxed.

"Would it be okay if we drove down there, Officer?" Julian asked. "I'm sure Brandi doesn't like to be seen riding in the back of your cruiser so often."

Deputy Little nodded. "Yeah. Okay. But you have to come now."

Julian turned and went to the SUV that had parked behind his car. He told Marduk, the driver, to move so they could head back out. Marduk did so with quick efficiency, pulling over onto the grass of Brandi's massive lawn.

"Can I have your house keys?" Julian called out to her.

Brandi reached in her purse and retrieved the keys, taking them over to Julian. He handed the keys to Marduk. "Take a look around, if you'd like," Julian told him. "Maybe you'll see something interesting."

Brandi almost took offense at that. She didn't want two strangers rifling through her things. But she knew they were here to protect her and if that meant becoming familiar with her house and everything in it, then she knew she'd just have to get over it. She decided she really didn't want to stand in their way in any case.

Julian took her arm gently in his hand and led her back to the sports car. He helped her climb in, started the engine and backed down the long driveway, putting his hand along the back of her seat as he turned around to guide his progress down the drive. Once on the road, they paused to let the deputy take the lead and followed him docilely into town.

When they reached the sheriff's station, Brandi turned to Julian. "Let me handle this," she said. "You're a stranger here. It might make things more difficult."

Julian looked as if he wished to argue. "All right," he conceded. "But if you need me, I'll be waiting right here."

Brandi smiled to let him know that his gesture was appreciated and got out of the car. Deputy Little fell into step beside her. "Who is that man?" he asked softly.

She'd known that Julian and his crew would be a noteworthy topic for the people of Mt. Airy. It was such a small town that anything unusual usually made the rounds of conversation. "Julian is a friend."

"Your boyfriend?"

"No." She chuckled nervously and licked her suddenly dry lips.

"And what about the other two?"

"They're friends of Julian's. Why?" She already knew the answer to that one.

"Just curious," he said, ears reddening. "I'm sorry if I'm being too personal."

"Not a problem," she said easily.

"Are they here because of…because of your monster," he choked out, face reddening further.

For some reason, Brandi felt the compulsion to lie to him about that. Really it was none of his business. And something warned her not to shake the hornet's nest. If the sheriff found out the real reason they were here, there'd be hell to pay. "No. They're just visiting from out of town," she lied easily.

The deputy nodded as if satisfied with her answer. He led her once more to the tiny interrogation room and left her with a wink and a smile. A few minutes later the sheriff came in with a small package in his hand and sat down in a chair across the rough table between them.

"There's been another disappearance," he said without preamble.

Brandi felt her insides clench with fear for the missing little one. "Why are you wasting your time by telling *me* this? Why don't you let the FBI handle this?" she asked incredulously.

Sheriff Adams cracked his knuckles. "So you're admitting there is a serial kidnapper loose in our town?"

"No. I'm just saying, the FBI should be involved. Sooner or later they'll have to be made aware of all this, if they haven't been already, and the longer you wait the worse it's going to look. Our townspeople can't keep this secret anymore. And maybe, if we're lucky, the FBI will listen to me. Maybe they can find a way to stop the monster."

Sheriff Adams sighed heavily. He put the small package he'd been carrying with him on the table. "I got this from your house today—don't worry, I had a warrant and you can see it for yourself," he assured her. "Do you know what that is?"

Brandi frowned. It was wrapped in brown paper. "Can I open it?" she asked.

"Go ahead."

She tore the paper open with unsteady fingers. Nestled inside was unlabeled videotape. She felt something insider her sink low, dreading what she knew would come next.

"You recognize that?" he asked her.

Brandi merely met his gaze silently.

"That there is one of your silly tapes. I watched it, and what I saw made my blood boil. How did you learn to make such realistic special effects? You never left town to go to college—you went to the community college here, and I know they don't teach the things I saw in the tape. How did you do it?"

"It's not special effects," she gritted out, ire rising.

"Is this tape an example of what you've been showing the people of this town, or did you make several different ones to make it all seem more legitimate?"

"I'm not lying to these poor families," she growled, anger steadily rising. "What you see on the tape is real. As real as you can get."

"I must say, you sound convincing even to me," he scoffed.

Brandi took a deep, steadying breath. "Look, how do you think I made the tape look so real then? I don't have the knowledge or the resources to fake something like that—you even said so yourself—and if you'd just think for one moment you'd know I speak nothing but the truth."

The sheriff sighed heavily. "I brought you in here to tell you that the Greenways lost their son Tommy last night. They're grief-stricken, as you can imagine. I'm warning you now that if you pull this stunt with them, even if they call you and beg for you to do it, you'll be thrown in jail until I can figure out something better to do with you. Understood?"

Brandi gritted her teeth against the urge to tell him exactly how she felt about his "warning". "Fine. Can I go now?" she asked, barely restraining herself.

"I'll be watching you," he said quietly. "I'll be watching you like a hawk."

"Whatever," she snapped. "Can I go?" she asked again, belligerently.

"Sure. Go. But remember what I told you."

"Yeah, yeah, I got it." She tossed the tape back at him, noting with satisfaction that he flinched. She left the room without looking back and stomped her way through the station until she was outside in the fresh air once more. She took a deep breath, but it did nothing to calm her frayed nerves. "*Fuck!*" She screamed out her frustration at the top of her lungs, uncaring that there were likely dozens of pairs of eyes watching her and listening.

Julian came to stand beside her, concern clearly written upon his handsome face. "What happened?"

Brandi caught her breath. "Nothing. Just that Podunk sheriff trying to bully me again," she growled.

"There's been another disappearance, hasn't there?" he asked knowingly.

Brandi frowned. "How can you know that?"

"I can see it written in the lines on your face," he said.

She took that in. "It was a little boy. For some reason this monster seems to like boys over girls. He's taken lots more boys than girls. Do you think that's significant?"

"Who can say? No one knows the mind of a monster. But I'd guess likely not. The monster is, for the most part, just a mindless entity set upon an evil path. It's probably just coincidence."

"Yeah. You're probably right," she agreed. She ran her hands through her hair wearily. "I just wish this thing would go away and leave our town alone."

"We'll stop it," Julian promised her gently. "We'll put a stop to all of this."

"But what about the missing children? Are they lost forever?"

Julian's eyes hooded. "I believe so. I'm sorry, but I don't think there's anything we can do to help them, if they even yet live. Bogles live in a realm beyond this one, feeding off life wherever it can. It's unlikely that any of the children have survived."

"Come on," she said with a heavy, heartfelt sigh. "Take me home."

Julian said nothing, opening the car door for her. He left her to her thoughts on the ride home and for that she was immensely grateful.

Chapter Eleven

Ramiel smelled the evil that still permeated the room. He was used to such scents, but this one rattled him. A child had been taken from this place. He would have known it even if he hadn't already been told.

Before leaving headquarters, Julian had briefed them on the state of the town and of Brandi, their seventh key. Ramiel had listened, but he supposed he hadn't listened hard enough. The malignancy that was prevalent in the house—more so in the back bedroom—both surprised and alarmed him. He didn't know how Brandi could even live here, much less sleep here.

He studied the video equipment and found himself impressed. The woman really knew her techno gadgets, that was for certain. There was no way the bogle could come through the gateway here without being caught on film. Ramiel marveled at the woman's courage and ingenuity in the face of such undeniable danger.

"I've searched the grounds. This place is a hotbed of evil," Marduk said, coming into the bedroom.

Ramiel agreed. "This was where the bogle first came through."

"That would explain it," Marduk nodded. "This house should be razed and the land burned."

"According to Julian, this is the only home Brandi has. If she can tolerate the darkness of this place, then we should as well. After all, aren't we also creatures of darkness?"

"Speak for yourself, Ramiel. I am a creature of light and always have been."

Lover's Key

"So you say," Ramiel smiled, flashing fang.

"Shut up," Marduk said, cuffing Ramiel's shoulder amiably. "So we're to watch this mortal woman. Do you think Julian fancies her?"

"Who wouldn't, with all that long, dark hair and those bright grey eyes? She's certainly easy on the senses. And besides, she *is* the seventh key. She needs guarding, don't you agree?"

"How can she be a key?" Marduk marveled for the hundredth time.

Ramiel shrugged. "I don't know. But I trust Julian's judgment. She must be a key."

"Do you know, I think this is the most I've ever heard you speak at once," Marduk chuckled.

"It must be all this fresh country air," Ramiel said jokingly, once more flashing his long, sharp fangs.

"So where do you think the missing key can be found?" Marduk asked, growing serious. "Any ideas?"

Ramiel sobered. "I haven't a clue. It could be anywhere. Anywhere in the world. It will no doubt take some time to find it, just as it took us time to find all the other keys. One thing I am certain of is that this will not be an easy quest."

"I feel the same thing, brother. And I don't like it," Marduk spat. "Not one bit. I'm ready to be done with this business."

"Are you afraid of opening the gate?" Ramiel asked.

"No. Why?"

Ramiel was silent for a long moment then seemed to shake himself free of an unpleasant feeling. "When the gate swings open at our command, all the evil that has been loosed in the world will be called back into the Pit. Are we not also evil ourselves? Will we not be subject to the gate's power?"

"I never gave it much thought before now. But I suppose you could be right. But then again, maybe not. Maybe the good that lies in our hearts will protect us somehow."

"I have no good in my heart," Ramiel growled.

"You don't think you do, but look at where we are. We're protecting a woman we don't know. We've sacrificed ourselves on the altar of fate to find these blasted keys. And for what? To save the world. Surely that earns us some brownie points, as they say."

Ramiel looked away, staring at the open closet. "I admit, I am fearful of the gate. I am a vampire, one of nature's darkest creatures. I belong in the Pit. It will surely call to me."

"But you are true of heart—you cannot deny it, for I have seen this in you. I do not think you will be at risk. And even if you were, do you think I'd let you loose into the unknown alone? Never, my friend. Never."

"We'll see," Ramiel sighed. "I cannot help but wonder, though. Especially here, where there is so much evil surrounding us. This town is rank with it. I know, in my heart, that the gate must be opened. But I fear for my own life—and yours—in the doing."

"We'll be fine, so long as we stick together. I'm sure of it."

"We'll see," Ramiel said again.

"Yes we will, and you'll feel foolish for dreading it." Maduk smiled in what he hoped was a reassuring manner. "Ramiel, no matter that you think so, you are not a bad man. I know your heart and it is indeed true. You have nothing to fear."

"I revel in what I am. I have never hated it. I am a vampire and I have never been happier. Surely that is a sin black enough to condemn me."

"You are a vampire, but you are not a killer. You never have been. And murder is the biggest black mark I know of that might stain anyone's soul. You're a Templar Knight now, just as I am. And everything that's holy about such an honor shall protect you from the Pit," Marduk said emphatically. "You've nothing to fear," he stated again, firmly.

"If you say so, then I shall believe you, my friend."

"I say so." Marduk smiled again, revealing a row of very straight, very white teeth.

Ramiel returned his smile. "I hear Julian's car approaching. Let's go out and see what happened to them at the sheriff's station."

Julian's car was actually a mile away—Ramiel's hearing was that acute. But by the time they made it out to Brandi's front porch, the red sports car had turned down the long gravel driveway. Julian must have been driving fairly fast.

Brandi was the first out of the car. Without a word to either man, she passed them and went into her house, slamming the screen door shut behind her. Julian got out of the car and went to stand beside his friends.

"The sheriff is being really hard on her," he explained.

"What does he want with her?" Ramiel asked.

"Brandi, bless her, has little guile. She's told the truth about the bogle from the first. Now the whole town thinks she's crazy and the police have seen the videotapes she makes of the bogle's visitations. They think she's staging them, to con something out of the victims."

"Why didn't she just lie about the bogle? She could have saved face if she had," Marduk observed curiously.

Julian shook his head. "I don't think it ever even occurred to her to lie about it. From the first, she's known that the bogle was dangerous. She's tried her best to warn others, but to no avail. No one wants to listen to her. No one in a position to do anything about it, that is. She's been stuck here on her own with this terrible knowledge for three years."

The trio was silent for a long moment, each wondering what it must be like to know the truth and have everyone think you mad because of it.

"We need to find the sixth key. Fast," Marduk said at last.

"I agree wholeheartedly and I'll begin searching right away," Julian said. "In the meantime, when I'm not around, I'm entrusting Brandi's safety to you two."

"We'll take good care of her," Marduk assured him.

"I'm going to head down to the café in town—it's the only place I know of with free internet access around here and I want to watch the townsfolk, get a feel for how they're living in this bogle's shadow. I won't be back until late tonight—I'm going to go ahead and explore this area as best I can before coming back. I want to know every nook and cranny of this place, just as well as Brandi does."

"What should we do in your absence?" Ramiel asked as Julian walked back to his car. "Is there anything we can do to aid you?"

"Do nothing for now. Just guard Brandi. Keep her out of trouble—that in itself should be a grueling job." He chuckled despite himself. "I'll do all the legwork on this one."

Julian left them standing there, climbed back into his car, revved the engine loudly then sped backward down the gravel drive.

Marduk and Ramiel eyed each other. "I have a horrible feeling that this is going to be a long night," Marduk said with a grin.

"Indeed," Ramiel sighed and turned to go into the house. "Damn. I never thought I'd end up a babysitter," he said under his breath.

Marduk merely laughed. "Come on, my friend, let's get Brandi to fix us up some grub, shall we? Well…for me anyway."

Ramiel chuckled, his voice sounding like the ringing of crystal bells.

* * * * *

Brandi felt a hot, wet mouth pull at her nipple erotically. She let out a breathless moan, a sound of surrender that shocked even her, and arched wantonly into the touch of that ravenous mouth. A large, warm hand ran down her body from neck to knee, petting her like a beloved kitten. A heavy weight rested against her, covering her, making her feel safe for the first time in three years.

The mouth moved down over her chest, lower to her stomach, and a tongue delved into the dip of her navel. Large, masculine fingers roamed all over her body, stroking and teasing until she was mindless to anything but the *feeling*. Her body quivered, aching for more of the delicious torture of those skillful hands.

Fingers plucked at her nipples as the hot mouth explored her navel. Her nipples felt hard as diamonds, as brightly hot as stars. Her sex was swollen and aching, wet and hot, begging to be touched. She'd never been so aroused.

The mouth lifted and she groaned her disappointment. But it was a short groan for the mouth settled itself over hers, tongue delving deep into her secrets, kissing her as she'd never been kissed before. A bubble of joy made her gasp into his mouth and tears filled her eyes, leaking from the corners to fall against her temples. It had been so long since someone— anyone—had held her in his arms like this.

She'd been so lonely, for so long.

If only she could fill her heart with love. Then she'd never feel alone ever again.

But what was love without trust? She could never love someone who didn't believe her, believe *in* her. It was unthinkable. Impossible.

Hands spread her legs, opening them wide. Strong, muscular hips settled between them, a huge, hard cock resting against her wet heat. But reality had intruded and Brandi bucked against it, trying to unseat her seducer. It was no good.

The cock fell into position and began to press inexorably deeper into her…

She awoke with a gasp, shooting upward in the bed.

Sweat soaked her and the bed. She shuddered, taking broken, ragged breaths. There was no one in the bed with her.

But the dream had felt so real. She more than half expected to see someone in the room with her, but it was empty save for her. Her nipples were still hard and her sex was aching, empty, bereft. But it had only been a dream. And dreams, she knew, faded eventually.

Brandi swung her legs out of the bed and rose unsteadily. She was dressed only in her over-large bed shirt and cotton panties. Grabbing a ragged terrycloth robe, she put it on and went to the door, opening it a crack and peeking out. There didn't seem to be anyone up and around out there. Brandi really didn't want to run into anyone in her present state of mind. But she decided to risk a quick trip to the kitchen for a glass of milk.

Her bare feet whispered across the floor. She almost immediately spotted Marduk, asleep on her couch. She tiptoed past him and into the kitchen. She opened the fridge, bent and retrieved the already half-empty carton of milk from the shelf. She knew she'd have to buy more in the morning. Damn. She truly hated going into town.

A noise caught her attention and she whirled around. Her nose bumped into Ramiel, who was standing but a few scant inches away from her. She unintentionally let out a squeak and backed into the fridge. "W-what do you want?" she asked nervously.

Ramiel's eyes glowed crimson, scaring Brandi down to her toes.

"You should be in bed," he said softly, his voice a gentle, melodic contrast to the look in his fierce eyes.

Brandi couldn't have agreed with him more. "I was j-just getting something to drink," she explained unevenly.

Ramiel nodded and, in the time it took Brandi to blink her eyes, he had vanished. She stood there mute for a long while then had to forcibly shake herself out of her surprised shock. She let out a shaky breath, opened the milk and drank straight from the carton, uncaring if anyone saw her doing it. Damn it, it was her house. She'd drink however she wanted, she thought stubbornly.

She heard a noise outside and cautiously went to investigate. She didn't want to run into Ramiel again—he spooked her too easily. But it wasn't Ramiel, and she breathed a sigh of relief. Julian stood on her porch, alone, leaning gracefully against one of the columns. The bright buckles of his boots twinkled in the moonlight. She opened the screen door and stepped out on silent feet.

"Why aren't you sleeping?" she asked him.

Julian turned his head and winked at her. "I couldn't. My brain is still going a million miles an hour."

"I know how you feel." She twisted her lips wryly.

"How about you? Why aren't you in bed?"

Brandi held up the almost empty carton. "I was getting something to drink. Want some?"

Julian held his hand out and accepted the carton. He turned it up and drank deeply, emptying it. "Thank you," he said, handing it back to her.

Brandi fingered the carton nervously. "You know, I've often wondered about the very first person to drink cow's milk. What that must have been like," she laughed. "What possessed him—or her—to try milk from any animal in the first place, let alone a big ol' dumb cow?"

Julian chuckled. "That is a puzzle," he agreed.

Brandi stood beside him, staring out into the darkness for a long while. "You know the guy who came out of my closet?"

Julian nodded and she continued. "Who do you suppose he was? And how did he do it, I wonder?"

"I think he's the one who stole the Hope," Julian said slowly. "But I can't be certain. It would make sense—any of the keys can allow one to teleport through the void of worlds if used for that purpose. But he would have to have some Templar blood in his veins or else the key wouldn't work. I don't know. It's a mystery. One I want solved as soon as possible."

Brandi wholeheartedly agreed with him. She shivered in the cool night air. Julian saw her and drew her into the circle of his arms. He gently turned her around so that her back pressed against his chest, and he rested his chin on her head, his arms enfolding her. He was so warm. She couldn't resist snuggling into his embrace.

He lowered his head and drew a long breath into his lungs. "You smell divine," he whispered against the shell of her ear.

Brandi shivered, and this time it had nothing to do with the coolness of the air around her. It seemed to have suddenly grown quite warm, actually.

"The moonlight becomes you," he continued. "It gives you a mysterious air that I find quite...appealing."

His arms tightened about her, holding her closer to him. Her nipples grew hard against his arm and she squirmed shyly. "You must be more tired than you thought," she said flippantly, feeling nothing close to flippant at all.

His lips whispered down to her neck and lingered. "Do you have any idea what you do to me?" he asked with a fierce intensity that made her knees go weak. "You don't, do you? God." His arms tightened and his body pressed hard against hers, his cock a thick, heavy weight at her back. "You've driven me mad." He pressed his lips tight to her neck and she nearly swooned back against him.

"Don't," she choked out, not even knowing what the word meant.

"I must," he whispered and turned her in his arms. He pressed a gentle, chaste kiss to her forehead and framed her face in his hands. He gazed deeply into her eyes and she felt her cheeks burn against his palms. His body crowded against hers, sinking into her, making her catch her breath raggedly. Her back was to the column now, the wood pressing into the skin of her buttocks and thighs.

Julian grabbed one of her legs and hooked it over his hip, opening her. He pressed his hips into her, his cock jutting into her softness, hard as stone. He dipped his head so that his lips barely touched hers. "I have to taste you," he murmured against her mouth and she gasped softly. He took the opportunity and claimed her mouth, his tongue searching deeply.

His hand roamed to her hair and fisted in its thickness, holding her still for his kiss. The other hand bit into her thigh, fingers sinking into her flesh with nearly bruising intensity. She moaned into his mouth and he swallowed the sound before tracing her lips with his tongue.

The hard planes of his body cradled her softness, as if fashioned solely for her and her alone. His muscular chest pressed against her aching breasts, his hips fit into the cradle of hers. His mouth opened over hers and she was lost. She slipped her tongue past his lips, tasting him deeply. He made a rough, ragged sound and crushed her tighter to him.

"I can smell your desire," he whispered brokenly against her mouth.

Brandi gasped. He caught her breath and gave her his own in return. His lips slanted over hers, his kiss growing deeper, imprinting himself on her.

A twig snapped loudly in the night beyond them and they quickly, almost guiltily, broke apart.

Julian took a ragged breath and the sound of it warmed Brandi's insides. It was moments before he regained his voice. "You should go get some sleep," he said roughly.

"You're right. I think I will," she said hoarsely. She turned and opened the screen door then paused, looking back at him. She closed the door firmly once more and turned to him. "Tell me something."

"What?" he asked.

"You say you're over seven hundred years old," she started.

"Thereabouts, yes."

"So what was it like, back then?" she asked curiously.

Julian smiled. "Simpler," he said. "Easier in some ways, harder in others."

"Do you miss the way things were?"

"Sometimes," he said thoughtfully. "But not always. You forget, I've had plenty of time to adjust to the way things have changed over the years."

Brandi thought silently for a long moment. "Sometimes I wish I had been born in a different century. Any but this one."

"Everyone feels that way at one time or another."

"I know. But I just don't feel like I fit in here, you know?" she asked.

Julian nodded. "You feel trapped by the circumstances surrounding you. It's no wonder you feel that way."

"I wish I could have seen things the way they used to be, back in the day," she said. "Just to have something to compare this time to."

"Trust me, you didn't miss out on much. One thing I've noticed is that no matter what time you find yourself in, it never feels like the right time."

Brandi smiled faintly. "Good night, Julian," she said, turning back to the door.

"Brandi," he said behind her, halting her. He faltered, seeming to be searching for the words and at last he sighed. "Sweet dreams," he said.

She went into the house without looking back.

Chapter Twelve

Marduk offered to come with her on her trip to the town's only grocery store. When she tried to turn down his offer to accompany her, he told her she had no choice. He had been instructed to keep her in his sight at all times, and that was exactly what he intended to do. She let him have his way, knowing a stubborn person when she saw one, and took him with her. But she didn't speak to him the whole way there, and he seemed inclined to leave her to her silence.

When they arrived at the store, Brandi immediately sensed that something was amiss. There was a small crowd gathered in the front of the market, an unusual sight to say the least. Brandi got out of her truck and walked over to the throng of people.

"What's going on?" she softly asked Mrs. Apple, an elderly, graying woman who was gathered among the others.

"Tracey Bib's house was broken into last night."

"Really?" Brandi asked, shocked. There hadn't been a robbery in Mt. Airy for as long as she could remember.

"Yeah. She came home from dinner and was changing her clothes when a man burst out of her closet and ran from the house."

Brandi's nerve endings went on immediate alert. "From the closet, you say?"

"Yes. He'd been hiding in there, probably watching poor Tracey dress like a dirty peeping Tom. What is this town coming to?"

Brandi cast a significant glance to Marduk, who silently nodded his understanding. They both knew this wasn't just a normal break-in. She knew it had to be the diamond thief playing with his newfound abilities. Tripping through the void, no doubt leaving all sorts of havoc in his wake.

At least it had been him and not the bogle to come through Tracey's closet, Brandi thought with relief.

She wanted to talk to Tracey, to ask her a few questions, but she didn't dare. Tracey was one of the people who thought her guilty of killing her nephew. No way would she speak with Brandi. No way would she listen to the truth.

Brandi made her way through the crowd, pointedly ignoring Tracey as she passed. She went into the store, grabbing a basket for her purchases. She picked up a carton of milk, remembered how Julian liked to drink it too and took a second. She grabbed a few other things, mostly junk food, some chips and nuts and doughnuts, and made her way to the checkout counter.

Marduk followed her every move, hot on her heels. It made her more than a little uncomfortable. Especially when she knew she was being watched by dozens of pairs of eyes—no doubt everyone thought he was her lover. She did her best to ignore him, knowing he was only there for her safety. But it was difficult. Marduk was not an easy man to ignore.

She found herself wishing it had been Julian to accompany her into town. But he'd left early that morning, according to Ramiel, long before she'd awakened. He'd left to begin his search for the missing key, and Brandi could only wait idly by until he found it. She hated that more than anything—her inability to do anything useful.

But she trusted Julian. She didn't know why. It was true she barely knew him—but she trusted him implicitly. She had no doubt he would find the missing key and that he would somehow help her put a stop to the bogle's reign of terror in her town.

She couldn't help but wonder if the bogle might strike again before Julian found the sixth key. Brandi hoped not. She really didn't think the town could hold up under the weight of another missing child.

Smiling politely, she set her purchases before the clerk and waited to be checked out.

"Do you suppose Tracey's intruder could be the kidnapper?" Melissa, the cashier, asked.

Brandi shrugged. "I don't know," she answered evasively.

"It might be. But Tracey doesn't have any kids so I can't see why the kidnapper would be at her house. Oh! Did you hear the FBI is in town? The sheriff finally called them in to help with the case."

Brandi felt her eyes grow wide with shock. "Really? I thought he'd never get around to doing that."

"None of us did. But we were wrong, thank the good Lord. They arrived here this morning. From what I hear they've got the whole sheriff's department in an uproar. They're none too happy that we waited so long to come forward."

"I told Rob a dozen times that he should call the FBI. I told him the longer he waited, the worse it would look. But you know how he is. He doesn't really listen to anyone but himself."

"He is a stubborn one, I'll give you that. But at least help has finally arrived. I'll be glad to hear what the FBI thinks of our situation," Melissa said.

"Yeah," Brandi agreed, taking her bags of groceries. "The next few days ought to be pretty interesting."

"Amen to that," Melissa chuckled. She nodded her head toward Marduk. "Who's your friend?"

"Marduk. Marduk, this is Melissa Holmes. She's one of the few people left who doesn't think I'm crazy."

Melissa laughed. "Well, not completely anyway," she teased gently. "What an interesting name, Marduk. What brings you here to our little town, hon?"

"Why, all the pretty ladies of course." He winked at Melissa and jerked Brandi close to him, hugging her.

Melissa laughed and blushed becomingly.

Brandi rolled her eyes and nudged Marduk away from her, precariously balancing the groceries in her arms. He reached over and deftly took her burden from her, carrying them so easily, as if the heavy bags weighed no more than a sack of feathers might. It was disconcerting, his easy strength, setting Brandi's nerves on end.

Waving goodbye to Melissa, Brandi grabbed a bit of Marduk's sleeve and led him out of the supermarket. She hopped into her truck, slammed it into gear and pulled out the moment Marduk settled himself into the seat next to her.

"What's wrong?" he asked after a few moments of very fast driving, voice pointedly mild and unassuming.

Brandi gritted her teeth. She hated having to explain herself, especially to a stranger. She'd been alone for so long it just didn't feel right. But she knew Julian trusted Marduk and she felt sure she should do no less. After all, he was here to help her, wasn't he? "I don't suppose you think the FBI will want to hear my side of things regarding those missing kids, do you?" she asked finally.

Marduk sighed and turned to look at her. Brandi kept her eyes resolutely forward on the road, but she could feel his strange amber eyes burning into her. She wondered idly if he could read her mind. It wouldn't have surprised her, not after all the things she'd learned in the past few days. Just to test it, she thought of something particularly ugly—the dirtiest word she knew, and she did know some doozies. When Marduk didn't react, she assumed that meant no, he could not read minds. That was a relief.

"Why did you feel you need to tell anyone about the bogle in the first place? You had to know that no one will believe you. Even if you had a mountain of evidence to prove your claim, I doubt seriously that anyone would believe without seeing the spirit firsthand. Why do you put yourself in the line of fire like this?" he asked with great interest.

It was Brandi's turn to sigh. "I...well, I..." She faltered and tried again. "I just have to tell the truth. That's all. Just because no one believes me doesn't mean I should keep the truth a secret from everyone. Besides, some people believe me. And maybe the FBI has some experience with these things. One can hope, right?" She laughed humorlessly.

"I doubt seriously that they have. This sort of thing usually falls into the jurisdiction of people like me and Julian and Ramiel. There aren't very many people like us who have had much experience with these sorts of problems, I'm sorry to say," he explained, blessedly taking his intense stare off her to look out the window.

"But it's possible."

"Brandi, I don't think that telling this to the FBI is going to help anything. Especially given the situation you're in. You've already got the sheriff of the town breathing down your neck. Do you want the Feds to be suspicious of you too? Because they will be once they hear your story. As it is, I'm sure you'll top their list of suspects anyway, once they find out what you've been doing here for the past three years," he pointed out.

Brandi growled and slammed her fist against the steering wheel. "What do you want me to do, Marduk? Huh? Do you want me to just stand back and watch while so much evil is being done around me? I can't. I *won't*. If the Feds come asking, I *will* tell them the truth. I don't care what they do to me. They'll all see the truth eventually, I'm sure of it. I *have* to be sure." Her words ended in a choked whisper.

"Even at the risk of jeopardizing our mission? One, I'm sure I needn't remind you, is of vital importance—not just for us but for everyone. We need you."

Brandi shuddered. "I just don't know what else to do."

"I didn't mean to upset you," Marduk said gently. "You're a strange human. I don't understand you. It's been my experience that people don't put themselves in the line of fire like you have. Not even for the sake of truth."

"Then you've been around the wrong people," she bit out.

"Maybe you're right," he conceded, sounding as if his own admission surprised him.

They fell into silence, both lost in thought, and Brandi made the last of the trip home at a more comfortable speed.

*****

That night, Julian returned to her home. He, Marduk and Ramiel went out onto the front porch and talked amongst themselves for a long while. When Brandi brought out glasses of sweet tea for them—could a vampire drink tea?—they fell silent, as if they didn't want her to overhear their conversation. Not that Brandi cared. She needed the time to herself anyway; she wasn't used to being around so many people.

She curled up on the couch in her sitting room and watched *Invader Zim*—her favorite cartoon—and ignored the murmured voices of her guests on the porch. It was dark outside and the crickets and bullfrogs made their loud calls to the moon, a music that always helped to calm Brandi's nerves. *Invader Zim* ended to be replaced by *SpongeBob SquarePants* and Brandi, despite herself, fell into a light doze.

She awoke with a start when the screen door that led to the front porch closed with a loud, resounding bang. Julian stood, towering over her, his eyes hard and serious.

"We need to talk."

Brandi sat up straighter and rubbed the sleep from her eyes. "What about?"

"Come outside with me. It makes me uncomfortable to be in here."

She nodded, understanding how he felt, and went out onto the porch with him. Marduk and Ramiel were both absent, but Brandi didn't know how far they had gone. "Where did the guys go?"

"I sent them on...errands."

"I heard that hesitation. Are you sure these errands don't have anything to do with me? I mean, you'd tell me if they did, right?"

"They're not to do with you—at least not directly." He gave her a lopsided grin, his teeth bright even in the shadowy dark. "They went into town for a while."

"Oh. Okay. Well, what did you want to talk about?" she asked, sitting down in her favorite oak rocking chair. He towered over her and she had to crane her neck to look him in the eye so she opted instead to stare out over the expanse of her front yard and the trees that lay beyond.

"I think I've an idea where the sixth key may be."

Brandi's eyes flew back to his face. "Sit down, why don't you," she growled and waited until he did so before continuing. "Where do you think it is then?"

He was silent for a moment, perched gingerly on his rocking chair, as if choosing his words carefully. He shrugged and took a deep breath. "I think it's right here. In this town."

Brandi was incredulous. "Here? But how?"

Julian shook his head. "I don't know. But I'm almost certain it is here."

"What are the odds of finding two keys in the same place?" she couldn't help but ask.

"Very remote," he answered.

"But where could it be? I thought you said it had been stolen."

"It was. And if my instincts are correct then the thief is here and he—or she—has the stone in his possession still."

"How will you pinpoint its location? Will you knock on every door in town?"

"I was hoping I wouldn't have to. In fact, I had hoped that you could give me some idea of where to start looking. But if it comes to that then yes, so be it, even if I have to visit every home in this whole town." His cool blue eyes were hard as diamonds.

"How should I know where you need to start looking?"

"You know this town like the back of your hand. Think. Is there anyone who you might believe could possess the stone?"

Brandi thought for a long moment. "No," she answered finally. "I can't think of anybody."

"Try harder. Think it over for the next couple of days while I and my men do our own searching. Sooner or later we'll get a break and when we do, we'll have all seven keys."

"What will you do once you have them?"

"We'll take a trip to Paris. To Montmartre, and Sacré-Coeur, the Catholic basilica on the hilltop overlooking the city. It's there, in the catacombs beneath the church, that we'll find the gate to the netherworld. There that we must make our stand against evil."

"Paris. It's so far away," she said as if to herself. "I've never been so far away from home before."

"It must be done," Julian said firmly. "We have no choice."

Brandi felt her lips thin into a tight line. It seemed she'd had no choices at all, not since her nephew's disappearance. Fate had a tight stranglehold on her. She wondered when, if ever, it would finally let go. And if she'd even be alive to see it.

"You're from France, are you not?" she asked.

"I was once. Long ago."

"I can still hear the trace of an accent in your words," she pointed out.

"Some things are hard to let go of," he said.

"Tell me about it." She chuckled despite herself. Brandi rose from her seat and walked to the edge of her porch, looking out at the stars. The night was bright, from the sparkling of the stars and the shine of the moon, and Brandi could see far down the yard and beyond into the trees that flanked her home. "Are you absolutely sure I'm the seventh key?" She had to ask.

"I know you are." Julian had walked up behind her and he now placed a large, strong hand on her shoulder and turned her to face him. "There can be no doubt of it."

Brandi tried and failed not to be caught up in his intensely blue stare. He had the most amazing eyes. Eyes a girl could drown in if she weren't careful. Eyes that could make a woman do anything Julian wanted her to, no doubt, and without any protest whatsoever.

Wait. She was being fanciful again. Something about Julian brought this out in her and she wasn't sure she liked it at all.

Julian's fingers trailed gently down the side of her cheek. She shivered.

"Your eyes look like smoke in the moonlight," he whispered, his cinnamon breath fanning across her mouth so that she could almost taste it. Both his arms framed her, resting against the porch railing at her back, penning her in effectively.

Brandi felt her pulse race erratically at his nearness. She tried and failed to drag her gaze from his. His unique scent, like Nag Champa incense mixed with the cinnamon flavor of his breath, entranced her and she caught herself breathing it deep into her lungs as if to hold him there inside her. His very being permeated her skin, her sense of smell and feel and taste. It was as if they were a part of each other already.

She wanted to touch. Oh how desperately she longed to reach out and put her arms around him. But she didn't. Couldn't. She was too afraid of what might happen next. Too afraid…and too anticipatory all at the same time.

She was in danger and she knew it. Whether Julian meant to be or not, he was too much temptation in just one man's skin. She ducked under his arm and darted away from him, trying desperately to catch a breath that didn't smell of him.

But Julian had different ideas. He caught her hand before she could stop him and pulled her to him. Closer and closer, until they touched from breast to knee. He was so tall, so big and strong, he nearly dwarfed her. Brandi felt as fragile as a moth caught in his flame, no longer able to deny the attraction of this magnificent man.

He rubbed his large hands up and down her arms, leaving chill bumps in their wake. Her breasts moved with her panting breaths, rubbing delicately across his chest until her nipples were hard and aching pleasantly.

"You don't know how alluring you are to me," Julian said, pressing his lips lightly against her temple, his breath fanning through strands of her hair. "I find myself thinking about you more than I should. You're interfering in my mission, my life. And yet you still have no idea how truly beautiful you are."

"I'm not beautiful," she protested reflexively.

Julian put a finger beneath her chin and lifted her face until her gaze was once more caught by his. "You are. But your beauty is so much more than just your lovely exterior. You have a beautiful soul within you, Brandi. A rare and magnificent thing that only makes me want you more. You take my breath away, lass." The French lilt in his words was heavy and pronounced.

She jerked her chin away and avoided his too-intense gaze. "You don't want me," she said, but her words were tremulous and breathless. "Stop saying such things."

"Why? They are nothing but the truth, something I know you hold in very high esteem. And I'm being as gentle as I know how to be. If I told you everything that was in my mind right now I'd shock you down to your toes."

Brandi swallowed hard, nervously, and put her hands on his chest, marveling at the rock-hard bulge of muscle she found there even as she tried — in vain — to push him away.

Julian pulled her even closer, until their lower bodies were pressed tight together. There was no mistaking that he wanted her. The proof of it lay heavy and hard against her belly. It made her lose what breath she had, making her dizzy even as her sex grew moist and heavy with need. Before she could hold back the revealing sound, she moaned breathlessly and immediately blushed beneath his heated stare.

"Are you married?" she asked, desperate to change the subject. "Surely in all the years you've lived, you've been married at least once."

Julian smiled knowingly. "I'm not married. Nor have I ever been — though I almost did once, long ago. Alas, it was not meant to be. I never met my soul mate, if that's what you're getting at. You're not going to get off that easy m'dear. No, I'm most definitely single."

Brandi swore under her breath. He was too cocky by half. But then, it was most titillating, this dance with words and small caresses. Julian was indeed a very slick fellow. He knew this game all too well and played it like the satyr he no doubt was and had been for hundreds of years. Brandi could only imagine how the women of earlier times had dealt with so bold a man.

Or maybe he was only this bold with her. The thought made her heart triple its fast beat.

Lover's Key

"I want you," he sighed and bent to kiss the shell of her ear, running his tongue along the sensitive ridge of flesh.

She trembled. "Don't say such things."

"Ah Brandi, my fearless one. You would brave danger with the darkest monster, brave the most damaging of reputations, yet it is I who makes you cautious. Very disappointing. But also very interesting, don't you think?"

"I'm not scared of you," she gritted out.

"Then what are you afraid of, hmm? Your eyes and your heart scream yes, but your mind says no to me and I want to know why. Do *I* frighten you or is it the thought of my possessing your body that frightens you so?"

"Shut up," she cried, finally managing to jerk away from him. "I'm not afraid of you. I'm not afraid of anything," she practically yelled into the darkness.

"Then you won't be afraid to search through the people of your town until we find the diamond." One corner of his mouth lifted in a cocky grin.

Oh but he'd played her well, she had to admit that. She'd almost believed him there for a moment. But no—no man like this could ever really want her. Not as desperately as he said he did, anyway. She knew it well, but that in no way diminished the disappointment she felt. He'd merely been steering her toward his main objective.

"You want me to just go door to door and ask for the diamond?" she asked, somewhat deflated.

"I want you to keep your eyes open and your ear close to the ground. There's bound to be something that will point us in the right direction eventually."

Brandi sighed and turned to go into the house. Julian caught her hand once more and turned her to face him. "I've upset you."

"No," she protested, lying. "I'm fine."

"I don't mean to rile you," he said gently. "But I can't seem to help it. When I'm around you all rational thought leaves my head."

"Don't start that up again. You got me to agree to be your snoop, there's no need to continue the charade."

Julian's cool blue eyes widened with something that looked close to shock. "You don't believe me? You think I said all these things to make you do my bidding? No. No, little one. I meant every word I've said here tonight. Every word. And don't you forget that, not for a second." Two of his fingers caressed the pulse that beat in her wrist. "We'll talk about this again, you and I. Doubt it not."

He released her and Brandi turned and fled into the dark recesses of her house, praying for her heart to stop its wild pounding.

It was nearly dawn before she slept and Julian kept watch on her porch all through the night. Strangely, it didn't make her feel any safer.

Chapter Thirteen
One week later...

❧

Brandi shoved her trowel deep into the earth and sat back on her heels, dusting the dirt and grime from her hands onto the thighs of her ratty jeans. She never worked with gloves, not in the garden anyway. She liked the feel of the dirt between her fingers. This go-around she was in her own garden for a change—not someone else's—and she was pleased with what she saw.

She had a healthy spread. Tomatoes, green beans, okra and corn. Carrots, radishes, and Vidalia onions—which wouldn't taste half as sweet grown outside of Vidalia, Georgia, but Brandi liked them all the same—rounded out the last of her crops. Each would taste fresh and crisp, grown to full ripeness beneath the warm Georgia sun. Granted the red clay was difficult to grow things in, but Brandi—luckily—had a green thumb and her gardens always yielded plenty of fresh vegetables to see her and some of her neighbors through the winter months. Brandi always shared her crops—it was good luck to do so after all.

And she needed all the good luck she could get.

Marduk was at her back, sitting in a lawn chair with an ancient-looking book open in his hands. It had taken some time, but Brandi was getting used to the presence of at least one of her male caretakers always at her side. It wasn't as if she had a choice anyway. They never left her alone except to sleep and use the bathroom—not one second.

So far there had been no sign of the sixth key and Brandi knew the men were getting impatient for news, any news, that might aid them in their quest. Brandi had done as Julian asked, keeping her eyes and ears open for any clues that might lead them to their quarry, asking people pertinent questions, listening to the gossips, but so far she'd learned nothing of any use to them.

The only development, as far as Brandi was aware, was that Julian had pinpointed a group of apartment buildings as targets to search through. He felt sure the jewel was there, but there were dozens of residents to question, to investigate, and he hadn't made much progress so far. Brandi's reputation had fast rubbed off on the three men—Marduk especially, since everyone now thought they were lovers, thanks to his behavior in town—and few of the townspeople trusted them enough to cooperate with Julian's peculiar questions.

Unbeknownst to her three protectors, Brandi still sat up each night in her nephew's bedroom, waiting and willing for the bogle to show up once more. But of course, it was to no avail. Whatever seal she'd managed to put on the doorway into the netherworld was a strong one that she had no idea how to break through. It was very disheartening.

The days went by lazily and uneventfully. She'd grown fond of Marduk, for he was an interesting and often charming man. Ramiel she saw very little of—she felt sure it was because Julian had warned him away. He was too much a predator for her liking anyway, so the bridge between them was a welcome one to her. And as for Julian…Julian rarely spoke to her anymore. He was gone from morning to dusk and they only really saw each other at dinner, where all conversation was kept polite and friendly.

It was driving her crazy.

After the passionate words he'd shared, Julian had closed up tight as a drum. He hadn't mentioned the events of that night on the porch, nor had she. But it was there between them nonetheless and every moment she spent in his presence seemed charged with such sexual tension that it nearly stole her breath. They both were well aware of it—this she knew for she'd seen the smoldering look of desire in Julian's witch eyes more than once—yet neither had dared acted on it.

Yet.

Brandi kept waiting for the other shoe to drop. For Julian to make another advance. For him to say or do something the least bit outrageous. Anything to break this strange truce between them. And for some odd reason she couldn't understand, Brandi actually wanted that truce to end. She wanted that intense, dangerous man she knew smoldered beneath the surface of his calm façade. She wanted him.

She could no longer deny it. Even if she'd wanted to, which she didn't. Whenever she caught sight of Julian, her heart jumped into her throat and her palms began to sweat. Just catching a faint trail of his intoxicating scent made her reel dizzily and it was all she could do not to jump him and demand that he take her on the spot.

But she wasn't so bold, at least not yet. Though given enough of this friendly, non-confrontational charade they were playing and she just might do it. She was getting that desperate over the situation. It was just too much.

The dark was gathering about her and she climbed to her feet with a wince. Her legs had gone to sleep. How long had she sat there, woolgathering? She dusted her hands one last time and went to make dinner for three—Ramiel, of course, did not eat food. In fact, as far as she knew, the Templars kept Ramiel well stocked in donated blood. She shuddered just thinking about it.

Marduk followed her into her house, far enough away from her that she needn't converse with him should she choose not to. Marduk was nothing if not diplomatically polite, she'd noticed. He sat in front of the TV while she went about preparing the meal. She made fried chicken, mashed potatoes from scratch and served up sweet corn from her garden. Soon the house smelled thickly of fragrant foods, and she told Marduk to fetch Julian from wherever he was so they could all eat.

While Marduk left the house, Brandi took the opportunity to go to her bedroom and check her audio and visual equipment. She made sure everything was working properly and efficiently. She opened the closet and went in, pushing at the walls, just testing to make sure everything was as it should be, and sighed wearily. She wondered if this nightmare would ever be over and knew that it wouldn't—not until she found a way to destroy the bogle.

And maybe, just maybe, if she were lucky, she'd find a way to save the children. If they still lived. Brandi bit her lip until it bled and left her darkened bedroom as swiftly as her legs could carry her.

Marduk came back with Julian in tow and they all sat down at Brandi's dining room table to eat. Conversation was scattered at best, but Brandi didn't mind. She knew it was because the two men at her table so enjoyed her food. They could hardly get a word out between bites and soon everything on the table was consumed. It warmed her heart to know they liked her cooking so well and it made her feel good to provide for them. They were, after all, her guests and she was nothing if not a country girl at heart—it was her happiest wish to entertain hungry men with great appetites for her edible efforts.

It was almost easy enough for her to imagine that these two men were here under different circumstances. That they were simply just friends visiting, as she'd told the entire town, which no doubt disbelieved every word she said by now.

But they weren't friends, though she was growing to like them both as such, and they weren't just visiting.

"Did you learn anything new today, Julian?" she asked, broaching the subject with resignation. Her curiosity always got the better of her.

Julian sighed and put his napkin on the table, reaching for the last gulp of milk in his glass. "Nothing of importance," he said and downed the last of his beverage.

"Do you still think somebody at Edge Water Apartments has it?" she asked.

Julian nodded. "I've already begun asking questions but I'm getting nowhere. It seems your reputation has already affected mine here and most of the people in Mt. Airy distrust me on principle, I think. It's going to take some time but I believe, eventually, I'll see or hear something that will lead me to the one in possession of the jewel. Of that I have little doubt."

"The longer we search, the more evil enters the world," Marduk pointed out, speaking around a mouthful of potatoes.

"I know." Julian ran a frustrated hand through his hair. "I know. But I'm moving as fast as I can. This town keeps its secrets—you know that simply by noting how long they waited to alert the FBI about the disappearances—and it's not easy digging up any useful information. The people here keep to themselves, and they don't like a stranger prying into their affairs."

"Perhaps I should go around asking some questions of my own. I'm more likely to get a straightforward answer than you would anyway," Brandi pointed out.

Julian appeared to think on her words for a long moment. Then he nodded. "Perhaps you're right. It certainly couldn't hurt."

Brandi rose and fetched more milk to fill Julian's glass. She refilled Marduk's glass from the pitcher of tea that was already on the table. She was a good hostess; at least she had that to be proud of. "I can start tomorrow if you'd like."

"I'll come with you," Julian said at once.

Brandi frowned. "It might not be a good idea. If the people I talk to see you, they might prove to be a little more difficult than if I went alone."

"I'm not leaving you alone," he said firmly.

Brandi put one hand on her hip and stared at him hard. "Honey, I've been by myself for a long time and nothing's happened to me yet. Chill out. I'll be fine without you."

"No."

She snorted. "Suit yourself then. But don't be surprised if we don't get anywhere." With that parting shot, Brandi piled up the now empty dishes—ignoring Julian's attempt to help her—and carried them to the kitchen sink. She spent the next twenty minutes cleaning up the greasy mess left behind from the chicken and loading the washer with her many dirty dishes.

It had grown dark outside by the time Brandi was finished and Marduk had left—no doubt to join Ramiel for their nightly expedition around the town. Brandi didn't know what they expected to find by roaming the night in secret but she was grateful that at least she wouldn't be forced to entertain them. She didn't feel much like entertaining at all tonight.

Julian was sitting on her porch, the last of his glass of milk cradled gently in his large hand. She went out and joined him, reveling in the cool breeze that blew tendrils of hair about her face, drying the sweat from her brow. "What are you up to tonight?" she asked.

"Waiting on you, actually."

Brandi saw the flash of his very white teeth. "Really? What for?"

"You know what for, baby."

Her heart skipped a beat. "You're not subtle at all, are you, Julian?"

"Subtlety wastes time."

Despite her mounting nervousness she laughed. It was so like Julian to think of such a masculine, arrogant thing to say.

"Come here," he said, voice husky and inviting.

Brandi moved until she was standing right beside him. "Is this what you wanted?"

Julian moved so fast she didn't see him coming. He grabbed her hand, jerked her to stand in front of him then turned and lifted her, settling her onto his lap. "That's much better," he said, licking the shell of her ear delicately, pulling her hips back so they were cradled by his.

The very real weight of his arousal pressed against her bottom like a brand and she had to fight the urge to undulate against him like a wanton. "What are you doing?" she squeaked, much to her embarrassment, as her pulse doubled.

"This," he said and put both his arms around her. He palmed one breast in each hand and kneaded the tender flesh gently. "And this," he said, letting one hand roam down until it was cupped warmly against her sex.

Brandi bit back a moan as his clever hands kneaded her into a fierce and sudden ache. "Julian." Her voice was a thready whisper in the gathering dark.

"Brandi," he returned, his breath tickling her ear. "You're shivering. Are you cold?"

She wasn't cold and she knew full well by the very satisfied tone of Julian's voice that he knew it too. "Stop teasing," she said throatily.

"I didn't realize I was teasing," he lied prettily. "I'm sorry. Would you rather I did this?" His hand slid up beneath her shirt and tugged at her bra until her breast fell free into his palm. "Or this?" His other hand opened the fly of her jeans and delved into her panties so that her naked sex was pressed tight against his kneading fingers.

"Julian, stop..." She struggled halfheartedly in his embrace. "The others might come back and see—"

"Easy, lass." He held her tighter against him. "They won't be back tonight," he said thickly, pressing a hot kiss to the curve of her throat and shoulder.

His hand plumped up her breast and his fingers toyed with her diamond-hard nipple. The index and middle finger of his other hand delved into the smooth, hairless lips of her cunt, seeking and finding the hard button her clit had swelled into. He pressed against her, rubbing her clit until she saw stars behind her clenched eyelids.

"Your pussy is so smooth. So soft." He shuddered against her back and ground his cock tighter against her bottom.

"I wax," she said breathlessly.

"I never knew it until now, sweet, but I'm a man who loves a bald pussy. Or perhaps it's just yours that enthralls me so." His fingers grew bolder, sliding in the wet folds of her flesh until they thrust deep into her aching channel. "Though I did so want to see the color of your hair here." Brandi tried and failed to hold back a ragged moan and she instinctively spread her legs wider, thrusting her hips forward.

All was silent but for the sound of their ragged breathing. Even the insects and woodland critters had fallen quiet. Brandi's hips began a slow, exquisite rhythm as his fingers thrust in an out of her trembling body. Julian moved her back against him in such a way that every movement her body made also pressed against his thick, throbbing cock, and soon they were both moaning softly with each rise and fall of their bodies against each other.

Brandi's whole body throbbed with each heavy beat of her heart. Her head fell limply back against Julian's broad, powerful shoulder and his lips trailed down the exposed line of her throat. He pulled a bit of her skin into his mouth and suckled it, leaving a love mark behind with his efforts that Brandi knew she'd have to disguise for days. The smell of evening dew, mixed with Julian's own unique scent, intoxicated her until her head reeled dizzily. Her entire being felt consumed, entranced by the magic that was solely Julian's. Electric desire danced throughout her extremities and created a gentle buzz that had her reeling drunkenly back against him.

"Julian," she gasped as her body rose toward that most elusive and most coveted peak.

"Shh. Let it happen, lass," he whispered wickedly into her ear, French accent thick as his fingers slid back and forth in the wet channel of her aching pussy. "Don't fight it. Don't fight me."

She felt like a stranger in her own skin. Her body sang like it had never sung before. No one, no one in her whole life, had ever made her feel the way Julian made her feel. In his arms, she felt aglow with such strange emotions that it felt like her heart might burst before she could get hold of herself. But control was something she never had when it came to Julian. She realized this even as she completely surrendered to the magic of his most skillful touch.

Riding his hand, undulating against his arousal, Brandi felt imbued with a strong magic that had nothing and everything to do with the pinnacle her body was reaching so desperately for. She realized that she had her eyes squeezed tightly shut and she opened them with a gasp.

Light.

Endless light.

Their bodies lay bathed in a brilliant golden light that reached in a circle around them, enclosing them in the protective rays of Julian's Templar magic. Brandi gasped and instinctively stiffened against Julian. But the fingers rolling her nipple made her gasp even harder.

"Julian," she panted. "What's happening?"

"You make me lose control," he said hoarsely against the skin of her throat. "Don't worry about it. My magic could never hurt you. *I* could never hurt you."

Brandi wasn't at all worried about getting hurt. At least not by the warm glow of his protective magic. But it felt so strange to be with this man, who was hundreds of years older than she, and so powerful that he held the secrets of the universe within the palm of his hand. Brandi had never believed in magic. Not even the bogle had swayed that belief. But Julian, without even trying, was showing her a world of magic that she had no defenses against.

His arms gathered her closer and his devilish fingers once again found her clit so that within seconds she was once more precariously perched on the very brink of the abyss of total ecstasy. Brandi moaned and let her body take its journey, bucking against the hand between her legs, rubbing her bottom wantonly against his cock.

Julian echoed her moan and shuddered at her back a split second before he sent her soaring into her own climax. They trembled weakly against each other, riding the waves of passion. Brandi's body felt boneless and once she could catch her breath, she collapsed back against Julian's chest. The light that had consumed them both faded and only the night was left behind.

Primitive terror consumed her as her body floated back to earth.

She was losing her heart to this man.

And there was nothing she could do to stop it.

Brandi tore his hands away from her body and surged to her feet. She swayed drunkenly for a moment as the last shivers of ecstasy rode through her. She shook her head to clear it and backed away from Julian, edging her way back to the door that would lead her into the dark cocoon of her house. "Don't ever do that again," she said in an expulsion of broken breath.

Julian's cool blue eyes fairly blazed in the darkness. "We both know I can't make that promise. And we both know you don't really want me to."

Her heart thumped hard and she shook her head, denying what she already knew was the ultimate truth. That she had fallen and fallen hard. "Just stay away from me, Julian." She backed up the last few steps to the door.

Julian rose from his seat. A dark wet spot stained the front of his trousers and Brandi couldn't seem to tear her eyes away from the sight. "You found pleasure in my arms," he said accusingly.

"I did," she whispered, unable to lie to him or herself. "But I don't want to do that again. You're too…too much for me to handle right now, Julian."

Julian's eyes never left hers, seeming to look deep into her soul. To escape him and her own traitorous desires, she turned and fled into the house without once looking back to see if he followed.

He didn't.

Chapter Fourteen

Déjà vu.

Brandi awoke to the sound of a fist pounding on her front door. She looked blearily around the living room and saw no sign of her three guests. She rose and went to answer her early morning visitor—she knew it was early yet because she'd barely closed her eyes to go to sleep before being jerked so rudely awake.

She opened the door and came face-to-face with two darkly suited gentlemen.

"Can I help you?" She shoved her hair out of her face blearily.

"Miss Carroll?"

"Yep, that's me," she said and sniffed. "Did I win the Publishers Clearing House drawing or something?"

"No, Miss Carroll, we're here to ask you a few questions."

"Who are you?" she asked suspiciously, seriously.

One of the men reached into the breast pocket of his blazer and drew out his ID. "I'm Agent Thread and this is Agent Perez. We're with the FBI. I was told you have a theory on who's behind all the disappearances here in Mt. Airy. I'd like to hear what you have to say."

Brandi barely bit back a groan of pure frustration. "Sure. Come on in," she said, stepping back to allow them inside. She wondered where Julian was—he'd never come in last night. She missed seeing him this morning.

She pushed thoughts of Julian and their last meeting from her mind. She'd need all her wits about her if she were to even attempt trying to explain the truth to these agents. And attempt it she would, even knowing there was no way these two men would believe a word of her story.

She motioned for her guests to have a seat in the sitting room and followed them in. "I suppose you've already heard my version of events from Sheriff Adams?"

"We did, but I'm not certain I understand all of the details," Agent Thread said. "The sheriff said you have videotaped proof of what *you* say happens. Can we take a look at it?"

Brandi snorted. "That was a very diplomatic way of putting it. Don't you mean to say that the sheriff thinks I'm a lunatic bent on conning something from the victims' families?"

"I didn't want to put it in such a way, but yes, you're right, that's exactly what he told us. Can you tell us anything different?"

Brandi took a deep, calming breath. "All I can tell you is the truth. My nephew was the first to be taken. I saw him being dragged by this big shadowy figure that came from the black hole that used to be the inside of Nick's closet." She swallowed and trudged on through the story she had told so many times before. "I didn't know what it was, but I felt such a primitive fear just from seeing it. What I saw taking my nephew from his room was nothing of this world, and I knew it right away. I immediately thought of the boogeyman." She sighed. "Well, the closet door swung shut before I could grab for Nick, and when I pulled open the door again there was no void in the closet, no way for me to follow the specter and save my nephew. But the next evening, after the cops had left and everything had kind of died down to a lull, I sat and waited in front of Nick's closet. I didn't know if anything would come through. But I wanted to try."

"Did something come through?" Agent Perez asked.

"Yes. The shadow came back and I fought it back with light. More than anything, it seems to hate the light."

"And you have recorded proof of this interaction with the...uh," Agent Thread cleared his throat, "boogeyman?"

Brandi nodded and went to her nephew's room to retrieve a few DVDs and videotapes for the agents. She handed them over, watching carefully for the agents' response. She knew they didn't believe her story—but she also knew they were very interested in her proof. Maybe they would listen to her, where the local police would not.

The two men rose from their seats. "We'll be going for now, but please, Miss Carroll, try to stay in town for the next few days."

Brandi nodded, expecting no less from them. "I'm telling the truth, you know," she felt compelled to say one last time.

"We'll speak again." Agent Thread shook her hand before he and his partner departed.

Brandi watched as they drove away and wished for the millionth time that she had never set eyes on the damn bogle.

* * * * *

Julian sat on the hood of his little sports car and looked up at the bright morning sky. He had driven most of the night, prowling the quiet streets of Mt. Airy until he knew his way around town like the back of his hand. And still, even after all the hours he'd spent eating up the road, he couldn't clear his thoughts of Brandi. Lately his thoughts had centered solely on the woman, and now, after last night, he felt completely obsessed with her.

He could smell her. On his clothes, on his hands and fingers. He hadn't kissed her last night. He wondered if he would have been able to keep from possessing her completely if he'd given in to the urge to take her mouth with his. Probably not.

Now he sat, parked in the middle of a great rolling pasture, far away from prying eyes, gathering his thoughts as best he could. It hadn't been easy getting the car this far, and he knew it would take a miracle to get him out, but right now he didn't care. Couldn't care. He had too much else on his mind.

When had this quest turned from finding the seven keys to seducing the seventh key in the flesh? He didn't know. But somehow, someway, he had lost sight of the bigger picture and focused solely on Brandi instead. He needed to get her off his mind. Needed to get back to the main goal and find the sixth key as soon as possible.

But how to exorcise Brandi from his thoughts, even for one moment?

His body was tense, wound up. He'd been in a state of semi-arousal ever since coming in his jeans the night before. He had cleaned up the mess of his weakness but it hadn't helped soothe his rampant libido in the least. In fact, the sight of his seed on his clothing had only made him want to spend the rest of his essence inside Brandi's hot little body.

A cool breeze toyed with his hair and he watched as a flock of geese flew overhead. One thing was for certain—the scenery this town offered was spectacular. Julian closed his eyes for a fleeting second and was assailed with the vision of Brandi's passion-drowned grey eyes. His eyes flew opened and he snarled a curse into the quiet of his surroundings.

There was only one way to get rid of this bear on his back.

He opened the fly of his jeans and reached in to free his thick, heavy cock to the caress of his hand and the cool morning air. He closed his eyes and let go, let his mind paint a vivid picture of Brandi caught in the throes of passion, as she had been last night in his arms. Her beautiful creamy skin had seemed to glow, even without his loss of control of his own vivid magic. She'd been magnificent.

With a groan, he palmed himself and began a steady, rhythmic stroke that he knew would soon help him dispel some of his pent-up aggression and passion. He imagined Brandi atop him, legs spread wide, riding him with a sweet, soft smile on her face and he groaned again. Would she tremble as she had last night, in thrall to his sensual mastery? Would her moans be soft and muffled or loud and exultant?

He vowed that one way or another he would find out. Soon. Else he ran the very real risk of losing his mind.

* * * * *

Brandi was weeding her front flowerbed when she heard the car pull into her driveway. She looked up, expecting to see Julian or one of the other men. But it was a police car that parked a few yards away from her.

"Deputy Little," she greeted him warily as he stepped from the car. "What brings you here, as if I couldn't guess?"

"Please call me Brian, Brandi. I just came to ask how your meeting with the FBI went this morning." The deputy flushed under her intense regard and Brandi looked away guiltily. She knew the deputy meant well, but she hadn't been able to keep from glaring at him anyway. She didn't want any more visitors today.

"Well, they didn't believe a word I said, as if you couldn't have guessed that on your own." She bent down and resumed weeding.

Brian came to stand beside her. She glanced over and saw the mirror shine on his black shoes and rolled her eyes.

"I watched the tapes you gave them."

"Good for you," she grunted and tugged at a particularly stubborn weed.

"I wanted you to know that I...that I believe you," he said haltingly.

Brandi stilled and looked up at him as he towered over her in the afternoon sunlight. "The hell you say."

"It's true. I had no idea, Brandi, I swear to you. I really thought you were lying. But there's no way you could have faked those tapes. No way that I can see, anyway. I just wanted to tell you that."

Brandi couldn't find words to express her relief that finally, somebody in her little town believed her.

She rose and swayed on her feet, blood rushing to her head. Brian reached out and steadied her. His hands lingered on her shoulders and she tried hard not to flinch away. "Thank you. For believing me," she managed finally. "It really means a lot that you do."

"What do you plan to do now?" he asked with no small amount of curiosity.

"I don't know," she said honestly. "We'll just have to wait and see."

"The FBI are naturally going to turn to you as a suspect," he pointed out.

Brandi sighed. "I know. There's not much I can do about that."

"They weren't hard on you this morning, were they?"

"No, not at all," she said with a frown.

"Good. I don't like them snooping around our town." He frowned.

"It's only been your town for the past three years," she chuckled.

Brian smiled sheepishly. "Yeah, well, it's easy to adopt this place as my own. And I like it quiet around here, don't you?"

"The quiet is *all* I like here anymore," she chuckled. "But I'll be glad when the FBI leaves. If they ever will. They aren't going to find the fabled kidnapper. What else can they do here?"

"Too much, if you ask me," Brian snorted. "But don't worry, I won't let them arrest you. Not when I know you're innocent."

"Thanks Brian, but I don't think there's much you can do."

"Well, if you need any help, just let me know. I want to see all this mess over with, the quicker the better."

"You and me both," she chuckled.

Brian bent forward and kissed her on the cheek. Brandi tried not to shudder at his unwanted advance and swallowed hard to keep her negative reaction to herself.

Something nagged at the back of her mind. There and then gone. Oh well, it would come to her eventually.

She pulled back from the deputy and shrugged away the feel of his fingers still on her shoulders. "Thanks for coming by," she said in an effort to see him on his way.

Brian flushed and stalked back to his patrol car. "Remember, give me a call if you need anything. Anything at all, okay? We're in this together now."

Brandi snorted to herself, nodded and waved as he got in the car and backed down her drive. When he was out of sight, she rubbed the feel of his kiss from her cheek with a grimy hand—she much preferred the dirt to the warm feeling his lips had left behind.

She stared off into the distance for a long while, thinking. After several minutes she decided to go inside and make a few important phone calls.

Chapter Fifteen

That night, the men conferred in her living room, trying to solve the puzzle of the missing diamond. Left to her own devices, Brandi kept returning to her nephew's bedroom, haunting it a surely as the bogle had years before. She heard them arguing and knew they wouldn't find the jewel, not unless they were really lucky. They knew the right place to look, but had no idea who might have it.

She knew. And it was time to put that knowledge to the test.

If she could call the bogle through the void, she felt sure she could call to the elusive possessor of the diamond. She readied all her recording equipment—even knowing that the gadgets probably wouldn't record much, if anything, of the coming moments. It was, by now, a habit that she do so.

Perched on the foot of her bed, holding her aluminum baseball bat, she looked at the closed closet door and tried to clear her mind. She wasn't certain how to do this, but something inside her told her she didn't need to consciously understand it. Instinctively she'd see this thing done, one way or another, she felt certain of that.

With a deep, heartfelt sigh, she focused solely on the closet door. She imagined her thoughts were a sword, slicing out into the distance beyond the physical realm. Imagined that the void opened up to her, letting her delve deep into its many ancient secrets. Black despair filled her and she knew instinctively that she'd touched the void at last. She concentrated harder, eyes narrowing, brow furrowed. Something heavy seemed to press against her lungs, cutting off her air supply. She gasped for breath, but was careful not to lose her focus.

"Come on. I know you're out there somewhere."

This time she didn't just want the bogle. She wanted the man who possessed the stone to come forth. He'd done it once before while she waited for the spirit, and she knew he could do it again.

"Please. Come to me," she whispered and it seemed that her words sped outward into the world before echoing eerily back to her ears. "*Come on.*" She gave a hard mental push, using all of her might to focus with searing intensity on the closet door.

Shocking cold filled the room. Brandi could see her breath mist out before her lips and shivered delicately, goose bumps tingling through her extremities. The smell of mold, old and stagnant, filled her nostrils. And a strange, silent breeze played with tendrils of her hair.

The doorknob turned, oh so slightly, and Brandi knew she had him. She rose swiftly, spreading her legs out to steady herself, raising the bat back up and over her shoulder. She took several steadying breaths, feeling the adrenaline rise in her bloodstream. This was it. She knew it down in her bones.

The closet door exploded open, flinging back against the wall with a resounding crash. The void, a black nothingness, stared malevolently back at her. Cold wind sucked at her, pulling her inexorably closer to the closet. She tried and failed to fight against the urge to take a few steps nearer. The blackness was absolute. Another world lay open before her. Seconds later, she saw a figure coming swiftly toward her and rushed to meet him.

The man in black fell into the room. Hesitating less than a heartbeat, Brandi raised the bat and brought it down on the backs of his knees. He collapsed onto the floor with a roar of pain and outrage. She swung the bat again, a mighty effort, and hit the back of his head with a shockingly loud *thwap*. He went down in a heap, no longer moving.

Brandi grinned savagely and bent over her fallen adversary. She reached down and pulled off the black mask the man wore. She had suspicions on who she would see there. Her suspicions proved correct.

"You slick bastard," she gritted out. She went to her knees, turned him over onto his back and saw the brilliant shine of the diamond on a thick, black silk rope about his neck. Its beauty blinded her for one dangerous moment and she had to look away in order to rally her courage further.

She reached down to take the stone from him.

"Stop!" Her bedroom door crashed inward, splintering. Without seeing him, she knew it must be Julian. He seemed to have a vendetta against all doors.

"It's Deputy Little," she said, endorphins kicking in, making her giddy and triumphant.

"I know. We were just at his apartment looking for him."

"I called him out," she said breathlessly.

"You shouldn't have done that," he growled. "You could have been killed!" His last words rose into a roar.

Brandi snorted. "I had to do *something*. Sitting around talking wasn't helping anybody."

"You court danger like many would court a lover," he told her. "You don't even know the meaning of the word caution, do you woman?"

"Don't talk to me like I'm a child," she growled, triumph turning to ire.

"When you act like one, how can I not?"

Brandi hissed and rose to her feet. "Fuck you."

"I'm too furious right now," he snapped back.

Without her consent a bubble of laughter broke free from her throat. It sounded hysterical even to her ears. "Why are you so bent out of shape? Nothing bad happened." She bent and reached again for the Hope.

Julian intercepted her, lifting her off her feet and setting her down farther away from Brian's inert form. "Don't touch the stone," he warned her.

"Why not?" she frowned.

"Don't you know anything about the Hope diamond? It's cursed. You mustn't touch it with your bare skin."

Brandi shivered. "It's really cursed? I thought that was just a legend."

"Believe it. Curses *are* real, and the one placed on this stone is very powerful and deadly."

Brandi's eyes widened and she glanced at the stone, this time warily. "I didn't know," she said unevenly.

"Thank fate that I arrived here in time to keep you from touching it," he said.

He turned toward the door. Ramiel and Marduk stepped into the room and, using a cloth to touch the stone, Ramiel removed it from around Brian's neck.

"You were right, Julian. I didn't think he'd be here, but you were right. How did you know?" Marduk asked curiously.

Julian shook his head. "I just knew. Leave it to our Brandi to find a way to weed out a thief."

The two men looked at Brandi. Marduk flashed a smile her way and Ramiel merely looked at her with his cool black eyes. "Good going, Brandi," Marduk said at last, holding the stone away from his body as if it were a dead animal.

Ramiel dragged the inert form of the deputy from the room. Marduk turned and left with him, closing the door behind him, leaving Brandi alone once again with Julian. She turned to the closet, expecting to perhaps see the void still there, but there was nothing, just the back of the closet staring back at her. "The way closed behind him," she said, disappointed.

"Did you expect otherwise?" Julian asked.

"Well, yeah, sort of."

"What does it matter now? We have the seven keys. We can finally put an end to this dangerous situation. The world will be safe, we'll see to that."

Brandi sighed. "Is the deputy alive?" She didn't really care and that frightened the hell out of her.

"He'll survive, but he'll have a hell of a headache when he wakes up." Julian turned to her, a dangerous passion burning in his eyes. "I thought I told you never to try calling to the bogle again?"

"I wasn't calling to the bogle. Not exactly. I was calling to Brian—Deputy Little."

Julian frowned. "How could you have known to call on him specifically?"

"Well, he moved here from D.C. I made some phone calls to the gossips in town and I found out he was a security guard for a museum before coming here. So I called the Smithsonian—that was the museum he'd been employed by. I knew it was all too coincidental. He was likely the one who took the diamond," she told him in a rush. "You know…" She searched for her next words. "I wonder why the curse didn't work on him?"

"He's descended from the Templars. He has to have had some arcane knowledge about him to achieve his trips through the void. If he had this knowledge, he surely must have knowledge of the curse. He no doubt used great care not to let the diamond touch his skin."

"God." She shook her head, marveling at how near she'd been to being caught in the stone's deadly curse. "So what do we do now?"

"We go to Paris and put a stop to all this evil as soon as possible," he told her.

"Paris," she breathed. "That's so far away—and I've never been out of the country. I don't have a passport or anything."

"But still we must go."

"Oh I know," she assured him. "I know. You're right. And the sooner the better. I don't want any more children to end up missing."

Julian pulled her to him with a forceful suddenness. Her whole body pressed tight to his, he bent and breathed deep of her hair. "Never do anything so foolish again," he warned in a throaty voice. "You frightened me near to death, woman."

Brandi couldn't find her own voice so she nodded her acquiescence instead, rubbing her cheek against the hard, muscled ridge of his chest. He smelled heavenly, like a sultry combination of incense, cinnamon and man. His scent fairly intoxicated her, making her knees weak and her heart race at a fast pace.

Julian took her face in his hands, tilted it just so and pressed his hot lips against hers. His thumb slid into the corner of her mouth, opening the way for his velvety tongue. He kissed her as if he wanted to crawl into her mouth and devour her from the inside. Nothing separated them, not even breath. The wicked glide of his tongue against hers melted her body so that she sagged against him and would have fallen had he not grabbed her up close against him.

His hands fisted at her back, lifting her shirt and baring the skin of her back to the cool air. Her body felt as though it burned, passion flowing through her veins in a storm that had her reeling drunkenly. She let her hands knead the thick bulge of muscle in his arms and opened her mouth wide for his kiss, giving him everything she had to give.

The ridge of his teeth caught the fullness of her lower lip and he drew it into his mouth to suckle upon it. Brandi's hands rose and caught in the silkiness of his dark, sexy hair, rubbing it between her fingers, marveling at its smooth texture. The hands at her back slid lower and cupped the cheeks of her ass, kneading them gently and lifting her up against him until the thick evidence of his arousal lay heavy against her own aching sex. She moaned uncontrollably into his mouth, uncaring that her feet dangled inches over the floor.

Julian's expert hands lowered her and pulled her shirt over her head before she even knew what was happening. He bent to his knees before her and took her breast—lacy bra and all—into his mouth. His kiss seared her, his suckling of her erect nipple through the lace made her catch her breath and tremble against him uncontrollably. His mouth made wet sucking noises as he moved first from one nipple to the other. He pushed the sides of her breasts together and buried his face in her cleavage, taking a deep breath of her scent. He rubbed his face against her, the rough stubble of his evening shadow beard scratching deliciously against her tender skin, leaving tiny streaks of pink behind.

Strong sensuality filled everything he did to her. He stood and lifted her again, so that her breasts were at his eye level. "Wrap your legs around my waist," he commanded. She did, hooking her ankles at the small of his back, moaning as he pressed his cock deeper into her softness.

The barrier of their clothing soon became a torture neither could bear. "Undress me." She panted the words before she even knew she'd meant to say them.

Julian planted her feet back on the floor and put his hands around her to find the fastening of her bra. A mere second later the scrap of lace floated to their feet. Brandi heard him gasp and her gaze flew to his. But he wasn't looking her in the eyes, oh no. His attention was held riveted by the sight of her up-thrust breasts bared for his pleasure. His hands reached out and cradled her breasts, testing their weight and texture, thumbs whispering over her nipples again and again until they were hard as pearls.

Brandi's own hands unbuttoned Julian's shirt and pushed it away from his shoulders. He paused in his adulation of her breasts just long enough to shrug it away. The sight of his bare chest made her pulse beat doubly fast. He was indeed a beautiful specimen of man. She'd known he was strong, knew he was built with bulging muscle, but she'd had no idea really how lovely he would be. His chest was large, his nipples dark. He had a smooth chest with very little hair, and this only served to make his muscles look even larger, stronger, more impressive.

He took her mouth again, sliding his tongue deep, tasting her every secret. His fingers plucked at her nipples, making her arch against him in invitation for a deeper caress. Every time he pinched or pulled at her nipples, something low inside her fisted then melted. Her body was a stranger to her. She'd never felt so aroused and there was nothing she could do to protect herself from that fact.

His fingers wandered down to the fastening of her jeans. In seconds he had her pants down around her ankles and she stepped from them eagerly, kicking them away with her foot. All she wore now was a scrap of pink—her thong. She had a moment to thank her lucky stars she was wearing sexy panties. Then Julian noticed them, going completely still against her.

"Woman, you're a menace," he growled. Surprising her, he went down on his knees again and pressed his face into the vee of her thighs. She felt the hot caress of his tongue through the thin barrier of silk, finding and pressing against the hard pebble of her clit until she was moaning uncontrollably, her hands fisted in his hair.

He hooked his teeth into the lace and pulled it down until he had completely bared her to him. "Woman, you have the most beautiful pussy," he said gruffly, staring. He buried his face between her legs again, but now there was no barrier to his wicked kiss. He licked her, sucking on the folds of her labia, using his teeth gently on her clit. Brandi would have collapsed onto the floor, but he held her up with his strong hands, making her enjoy every second his mouth played with her pussy.

"Take off your pants," she managed between moans and gasps.

Julian chuckled against her, the sound vibrating her clit so that Brandi let out a little screech of surprise. With one last, lingering kiss, he rose and did as she bade, shucking himself of his jeans and black underwear in record time.

He had the largest dick she'd ever seen. Long and thick—holy god he was thick—its tip glistened with pre-cum that Brandi longed to taste.

"Hurry," she said, reaching for him again.

He lifted her up and she wrapped her legs around him again. He took them both to the floor, gently laying her beneath him. He settled easily between her legs with her ankles hooked behind his back, holding on for dear life. His hands reached beneath her, cupping the cheeks of her ass, pulling her impossibly closer against him.

"Are you ready, lass?" he asked, bright blue gaze probing hers.

Brandi could only nod, then gasp as he positioned the head of his cock against her opening. He was so large—larger than she'd guessed. He slipped into her, stretching her impossibly, and Brandi cried out.

"Did I hurt you?" he asked, concerned, body going absolutely still over hers.

"No," she gasped. She dug her nails into the muscles of his ass. "Don't stop."

With a feral grin that displayed his very white teeth—reminding Brandi of the wolf in *Little Red Riding Hood*—he dipped and took one of her breasts deep into his mouth. He rolled her aching nipple around with his tongue and teeth, causing her to arch against him, which in turn caused his massive cock to impale her a little deeper. They both groaned. Julian moved his hips, undulating them, and he was sliding deeper into the heart of her. It hurt a little, but the pain only served as a potent aphrodisiac that made her want all he had to give her.

He was only a quarter of the way in, she guessed. Brandi wanted all of him, buried to the hilt inside her body. She wriggled and writhed beneath him, but it seemed Julian wanted to take his time. She was frantic by the time he started sliding even deeper into her. "Yes," she moaned helplessly, holding his head to her breast as he continued to suckle her.

"Be ready, lass. Here I come," he warned her. Before she could think of a reply, he thrust into her, hard, stretching her beyond limits, until he was seated balls deep in her wet, welcoming heat. "That's it. Take all of me, baby." He gave her a few moments to adjust to his body's invasion, and when he felt her muscles soften against him, melt and welcome him, he began a slow ride between her widespread legs.

"Oh *god*," she gasped and moved with him, undulating her hips against him until he, too, was groaning out an oath between clenched teeth. A bead of sweat fell from his brow onto her lips and her tongue darted out to capture its salty flavor.

They rocked together, hips moving like water in the same rhythm, their gasping breaths the only sound to break the silence. He rolled his hips and his cock, so deeply buried, rubbed wickedly against her G-spot. Brandi saw stars and cried out wildly, digging her nails into his wide, strong back and shoulders. He repeated the caress again and again, until Brandi's skin felt as if it might split asunder. She'd never felt this way, never even dreamed it was possible. It was making her mindless to everything but the feel, taste and scent of this man who held her as if he might never let her go.

The motions of his body grew faster, more desperate, and Brandi welcomed the strength and speed of his thrusts deep into the center of her being. She marveled at the strange yet completely right feeling of being in his arms, being ridden like a wild stallion might ride a mare. Nothing could have prepared her for the sheer, splendid reality of Julian's possession.

Julian put one of his fingers in his mouth and brought it out glistening with his saliva. Then he reached beneath her and gently slipped that finger into the moue of her anus. Brandi shrieked, but in surprise, not revulsion. It felt too wonderful to shock her for long and she relaxed beneath him, feeling his cock move so fluidly in and out of her while his finger thrust into her very sensitive flesh.

He lifted her, just so, so that her pelvis tilted up dramatically and this allowed him to slide even deeper into her body with each thrust. Brandi felt the breath leave her in a rush. Her scalp tingled, her lips felt passion-swollen and her breasts bounced against his chest, teasing her nipples to aching hardness with each movement of skin on skin.

It was too much.

Brandi let out a harsh cry as her body tightened, trembled and heated. She bucked underneath him, demanding a deeper penetration. Julian moved faster against her, slamming into her until their body made wet sounds with each thrust and withdraw. With one last, mighty shove, he penetrated her ass deeply with his finger and sent her soaring.

Screams reached her ears and she realized they were hers. But there was no stopping them — her body felt like a million stars exploded into space and screaming was all she could do to stay sane. She felt Julian shudder against her with a grunt, and she felt the searing hot splash of his cum hit her womb.

His movements slowed and gentled. Their bodies were wet with sweat and cum, sliding decadently against each other. Their heavy breathing eventually slowed and Julian collapsed onto her, his weight a welcome thing as she cradled him close. Tears seeped from the corner of her eyes and she realized that more than just sex had happened here. They'd been as one for those brief moments of lust. Complete and together. They had made spectacular love there on the floor of her bedroom…and she knew that nothing would ever be the same again.

Chapter Sixteen

ഇ

Julian, already fully dressed, nudged her awake. She was asleep on her floor—Julian had put a blanket over her to protect her nudity and she was grateful—and it couldn't have been a half-hour since they'd made love. She could still feel the shadow of him inside her, filling her deep. She must have fallen asleep shortly after, for she didn't remember much of anything after their lovemaking. "What is it?" she mumbled blearily.

"We can't sleep here—I hate the dark stain on this house. Come on. I have the perfect place." He helped her to her feet and bundled the blanket around her. "No, don't try to get dressed. Stay like you are. I like knowing your delectable body is bare beneath that flimsy barrier." He smiled and it was a tender smile she'd never seen on his face before. The knowledge that she had put that tenderness there warmed her insides.

Brandi and Julian ducked their heads outside the bedroom and, seeing no one, they crept out of the house and headed for Julian's waiting car. He bundled her into it, opening the door for her and tucking the cover around her protectively. He shut her door and walked around to his side of the car, climbing in, folding his long legs so that he could fit into the small vehicle. He started the car and backed it down the long driveway.

"Where are we going?" she asked. "There's only one hotel in town and that's Lisa Green's bed and breakfast. Trust me, we don't want to show up there together—it'll be all over town tomorrow."

"We're not going to a hotel," he told her with a wink.

Brandi knew better than to ask exactly where they were going. It was obvious by Julian's demeanor that he wished to surprise her. So she settled back in her blanket cocoon and enjoyed the drive, trusting him implicitly.

The night was well underway and no one was about. The roads were deserted and what few houses they passed all had darkened windows. It was eerily calm, and the darkness was absolute but for the beacon of Julian's headlights illuminating their way. They drove for long minutes, putting mile upon mile behind them. Brandi sank into a light doze, soothed by the rumbling of the car's engine and the welcome presence of Julian beside her.

When the car stopped, Brandi was shocked to see, by the digital clock in the car's dashboard, that they had been driving for almost an hour. She wondered where they could possibly be and tried to look out beyond the darkened window, but could see nothing in the impenetrable night. "Where are we?" she asked.

Julian ran his hand over her hair, brushing it out of her eyes. "Somewhere special," he whispered before laying his lips against the side of her throat. Brandi leaned into the caress and nearly fell over when Julian pulled abruptly away and exited the car. She snorted her disappointment and reached for her own door handle, but Julian beat her to the punch, opening it for her, taking her hand and aiding her out of the low-riding car.

He kissed her hand and looked deep into her eyes. "I want to show you something," he told her. He put his arm around her and led her deeper into the night. From the ground at their feet, Brandi knew they were in a pasture, far off the beaten path. In fact, looking behind them, Brandi couldn't see the road and no noises of passing traffic reached her ears. They must, indeed, be secluded out here.

The idea had some fabulous possibilities. She nearly giggled.

Julian reached ahead of them and made some swirling designs in the air with his fingertips. A bright flare of golden light exploded, blinding her. The brightness surrounded them in a circle, moving in symphony with each step they took, lighting their way. The glow of light was warm and welcoming. Brandi smelled the strong scent of cinnamon in the air, and knew that Julian's magic carried the very essence of him within it. She breathed deep of the scent, mingled with the crisp country air, and sighed happily.

They walked down a large, grassy hill to a tiny valley where a babbling brook welcomed them. Brandi's bare feet sank deep into the soft grass and the cool breeze in the air toyed with her long, heavy hair. Crickets chirped and bullfrogs croaked, so that the air around them was alive with sound. The trickling sound of the brook reached her ears, a most beautiful and uplifting music. She'd never felt so close to nature as she did now, and she'd grown up in green country, lived there all her life. But this was different. So different that she was speechless with awe. The night was alive with magic.

Julian traced more designs into the air before them and their golden circle of light spread out farther over the land. Brandi felt a strange sort of electricity tickle over her, causing her flesh to break out in goose bumps and the hair on the back of her nape to stand erect. Julian pulled her close and leaned down to capture her mouth. The bright gold of his magic flowed from his mouth into her, illuminating her from the inside. Her eyes were momentarily blinded by the light. Her whole being felt warm and giddy as she was drowned in his strange power.

Julian kissed her as if he would eat her alive, using his lips, teeth and tongue to pleasure them both. Brandi couldn't catch a breath — he had stolen it from her. Then he breathed for her, into her mouth, filling her lungs with the scent and taste of him, and the black spots that had begun to dance at the corners of her vision faded away. She gasped and opened her mouth wider as his kiss grew more and more passionate, giving herself to him completely, without restraint.

Her blanket fell away and her body was bared to the cool kiss of the night breeze. She'd never been naked outside, not since she was in diapers, and it felt deliciously wicked to be so now, here in Julian's arms. Her hair tickled her breasts until her nipples stabbed demandingly into Julian's chest. Brandi broke the kiss and Julian's lips wandered down her jaw, to her throat. She tore at his clothes, needing him to be as naked as she. His shirt fell away, buttons popping and flying in every direction as she jerked the material impatiently. With a sigh, she sank into his large, bare chest and nuzzled his pecs with her mouth.

Julian groaned and held her tight against him, squeezing her once before letting her go. She nearly stumbled without his arms around her, but she was relieved at once to see his hands move to the fastening of his trousers, removing them with swift, efficient motions.

When he was as nude as she, he lifted her and gently put her down in the middle of the brook. The water reached up to her calves, so cold it took her breath away, and she couldn't hold back a gasp. Julian stood before her, watching her, water swirling around their legs playfully, and a beautiful amber glow lit his eyes, warming her insides.

"Water is the blood of the Earth, did you know that?" he whispered.

Brandi shook her head.

Julian reached for her and pressed her length against his. "My power is greater out here where nature thrives," he told her. The light that surrounded them blazed with a sudden, searing intensity. He lifted her easily, as if she weighed no more than a feather, and urged her to wrap her legs around his waist. She did, and sighed blissfully when his cock pressed hard against her vulnerable sex. "I'm so strong right now that I could easily crush you," he said, words tickling over her throat with his breath. "But you have nothing to fear from me. I'll always keep you safe," he vowed. "Even from myself." He grinned wickedly.

A strong wind, redolent with the scent of green, growing things, blew over them, ruffling their hair. His long, dark hair tangled with hers, binding them together.

"Make love to me," she whispered against his mouth, darting her tongue out to taste him.

Julian kissed her mouth and lifted her up higher against him. Her breasts bobbed in front of his face and he bent to take one of her nipples into his suckling mouth, taking her flesh deep, tonguing and nibbling until she was once more breathless in his embrace.

He shifted her against him and began to penetrate her with his cock. Brandi gasped and writhed uncontrollably against him. Her clit was swollen and aching, pressed tight against him as he sunk in deep.

"*Oh god*," she gasped, feeling him deep inside, a part of her. "*Oh god*."

"Ride me," he commanded, his French accent thick. He put his palms beneath the fullness of her ass and lifted her. "Ride me and find ecstasy, love."

Brandi, with the aid of Julian's hands, began a slow thrust and withdrawal of her hips. She was so wet that their bodies made erotic liquid sounds with each movement of skin on skin. His cock was so large that it stretched her beyond limits, but Brandi welcomed the fullness. She had never felt as whole as she did now, in Julian's arms, and she wanted to catalogue every nuance of feeling to cherish in her memory in the days to come.

Julian took over, thrusting harder into the heart of her. He groaned and suckled her nipple demandingly. His fingers dug into the flesh of her bottom, lifting and separating her, making her vulnerable to the curiosity of the breeze. She cried out and felt her body clamp down hard on his thick cock. It was the headiest moment, unlike anything she knew. She was mindless as lust took over, driving them both into a frenzy.

"Harder," she panted. "Harder, *please*."

Julian growled and obliged her, pounding into her with such force that her teeth clicked together. She bit her tongue, bringing blood, but welcomed the pain as she welcomed each demanding thrust from her lover's body. Julian took her mouth in his, tasting her blood—the very essence of her—kissing her so deeply he seemed a part of her. An extension of herself.

Golden light blinded her. Electric energy danced over her skin, until it was so sensitive that the very air nudged her toward release. She took a breath and was drowned in the scent and taste of cinnamon on the breeze that still played about them. Her body felt swollen, ripe and ready for climax. Her clit ground against him as he thrust up into her and she was lost.

She heard Julian cry out, felt him pulse hotly within her, filling her with his cum. Her climax took her so hard and so deep that she couldn't open her eyes to see, to watch her love's face as he came. But she felt him, inside and out, smelled him, tasted him, and that was enough. Her body was alight with an inner flame that rivaled that of the golden protective light of Julian's magic still surrounding them. The breeze played over them like the tickle of a thousand loving fingers. The babbling brook played a wild, uninhibited music that entranced her. Everything in that moment was perfect.

Absolutely perfect.

Brandi felt her lips stretch with a pleased, excited grin. She laughed, feeling the last of Julian's tremors deep inside her. She had never felt so happy. She laughed again, unable to stop herself, and she clutched Julian tight to her, never wanting to let go. Julian joined her laughter, as breathless as she was, and twirled them in circles, splashing water about, holding her tight to him. "You please me, woman," he grunted. It was the most romantic moment of her life. She laughed again and he caught the sound with his mouth, kissing her soundly. "You please me very much," he said, grinning, words lilting like music.

They held each other tightly for a long, languorous moment. Droplets of water splashed on their skin, water that had nothing to do with the brook at their feet. Brandi looked up and saw the moon obscured by deep, dark clouds. A sound of thunder hit their ears and seconds later it began to rain.

Julian let her down and went to get her discarded blanket from where it lay on the grass. He came back and wrapped her in it, lifting her up against him like a child. He carried her to the car as the rain beat down upon their heads. "We'll sleep here tonight, with the sound of the rain to soothe us," he said, settling her back inside the car.

"Julian," she whispered after long moments had passed.

"Yes?" he whispered back, his breath fanning her hair.

"How did you come to be a Templar?" she asked, curious.

"When I was a young boy, I was the third of seven children. My family wasn't poor, but neither were we rich. I was sent to Notre Dame to study in the ways of the clergy. I trained from my fifth year into my early twenties to become a monk in the great church. It was common for males in my position to take up such training."

"Then what? How did you become a Knight after spending so much time preparing to take vows?" she pressed.

"I and many others were to take a pilgrimage to Jerusalem. Along the way our group was overtaken by bandits. Many of my brothers of the cloth were killed. I killed one of the brigands with my bare hands and took up his sword as he fell. I took to the sword as if born to it, fending off our attackers, but not before many died. I had never taken a life before. I was in shock. I wandered alone for days. Then, when I was in my deepest despair, knowing I could never devote my life to the church after my sins, a group of Templars found me. They had been searching for me since the attack. Gregori was one of the Knights. He took me under his wing and trained me in the ways of the Templars. I was a warrior from then on out."

"You lived in such a violent time," she said, marveling at his story. "I just can't see you as a monk."

Julian laughed, the sound shaking his chest, vibrating it against her breasts. "It wasn't meant to be. My destiny lay elsewhere. I knew it the moment I took the life of my first enemy. After that, there was no denying where my path in life lay."

"I can imagine," she said blithely, a smile tugging at the corners of her mouth. "You're full of surprises, Julian."

"I try to keep you guessing."

Brandi's laughter died down to a smile and she felt sleep tug at her, enfold her and consume her. The last thing she saw was the warm golden glow that still surrounded them, and Julian's love-softened eyes as they went to sleep looking at each other.

* * * * *

When they returned to her house, Brandi was startled to see Ramiel waiting for them. She blushed to the roots of her hair and gathered her blanket tighter around her, passing him on the porch as she went inside to find more decent clothing. But before the door had shut behind her, she heard Ramiel's whisper to Julian, "She smells of you..." Brandi's blush intensified.

Brandi went to her wardrobe and dressed, and for the first time in three years she didn't bother to check her video surveillance equipment. She pointedly ignored the closet. Ravenous, she went to the kitchen to find something to eat. After a long night and morning of lovemaking, Brandi needed quick energy. She grabbed a banana and wolfed it down in seconds, following it with a generous swig of milk straight from the carton. She could hear Julian and Ramiel murmuring out on the porch and decided to leave them to their privacy.

Something shimmery caught the corner of her eye. She looked at the kitchen table and gasped to see the Hope diamond sitting there, winking at her. Why the hell hadn't Ramiel and Marduk taken the stone to their headquarters? Perhaps they hadn't felt like taking the long drive... She eyed the diamond hungrily.

Would it be possible? *Could* it?

Her fingers itched to touch the stone, but she remembered just in time to grab a rag from the sink before picking it up. It twinkled in the morning sunlight, casting an array of rainbow hues on the ceiling that blinded her. Brandi took a deep breath to calm the sudden thudding of her heart, and clutched the stone to her breast.

She was descended from Templar Knights, just as Deputy Little had been. She knew it would work. It had to.

There was an ache in her heart as she realized just how angry and hurt Julian would be if he knew what she planned. But she was afraid he would keep her from doing what she was certain had to be done. It was foolhardy and dangerous, but so much tragedy had befallen her hometown and if she could lessen it in any way, or even bring a touch of understanding to the situation, she had to try.

Sprinting to her bedroom, Brandi went straight to the closet and threw open the door. She gripped the diamond in her fist and tired to focus her will. "Open for me," she whispered over and over beneath her breath. "Open *now*."

Nothing happened.

Several minutes elapsed.

"Open for me." She made it a mantra, repeating the words again and again.

Still, nothing happened.

With a disgusted growl, Brandi slammed the closet door shut again. "Fuck," she spat. "Why won't you open already?"

There came a rustling noise from inside the closet. Brandi felt her breath catch. Her hand slowly rose to the doorknob once more and turned it. She eased the door outward a sliver.

A black, shadowy hand darted out to grab her.

The closet door flung open wide and Brandi was in the grasp of the boogeyman. Its baleful touch sickened her, making her feel icy cold throughout her body. She grasped the stone and instinctively flung it up before the monster's face, wincing as it screamed and fell back, disappearing into the void.

Brandi took one last deep, steadying breath and plunged in after it.

Chapter Seventeen

It was darker than the deepest pit of hell. For several breathless moments, the dark was impenetrable. It was so absolute that Brandi lost sight of the opening of the closet at her back—the morning sunlight that had streamed through her bedroom windows faded out, replaced by the blackness of the void. There was no way out.

"Don't panic," she warned herself. Her words echoed in the stillness. "Just stay calm and try to find the kids. Then we'll worry about how to get back." She knew—she just *knew*—that she would find the missing children here somewhere. Beyond logic and beyond reason, she felt her purpose here strongly. She'd find those kids. Terrified and weakened no doubt, but still alive. She'd known it all along. If only she could keep her own terror at bay she might, at last, find them here. She took a blind step forward, then another and broke out into a stumbling run.

"Kids!" she cried out. "Nick! Where are you, baby? Speak to me. It's me, Aunt Brandi. Nick!"

Time passed. How much, Brandi couldn't guess. It felt like hours. She ran until she had a stitch in her side and her lungs breathed smoke. Grasping the jewel in her hand so tightly that her knuckles were no doubt bone white, she faltered and paused to catch her breath.

"Nick," she called out, over and over. But there was no answer.

She turned in circles, unable to catch her bearings. "Dammit, Nickolas Andrew Dill, answer me!" she thundered.

There came a noise from deep within the blackness.

It was small, but she definitely heard something. She ran blindly, hoping she was headed in the right direction, when the sound came again, ahead of her, and she began to sprint. It was more than a little disorienting, not being able to see anything in front of her, even the ground her feet audibly slapped on. She'd never seen such total...*nothingness*.

Tendrils shot out in the darkness, grabbing and enveloping her. Brandi felt the icy touch of the bogle and screamed. Her mouth felt the cold touch and something inside her wrenched painfully. She felt her strength drain and knew the bogle was feeding on her, leeching out her life force. She struggled with every ounce of strength left in her body, wrenching herself from the monster's grasp, bumbling awkwardly away from it as fast as her feet could carry her.

She ran straight into a large, hard body and fell flat on her butt with a sob.

"Woman, have you no sanity?!" Julian's words were the most welcome she'd ever heard in her life.

"Oh Julian! Help me. We have to find the kids!"

"Brandi," he said gently, righting her with steady hands "I don't think they're here. They've been used up. The bogle wouldn't let them survive for so long."

"I don't believe you," she panted. She grasped blindly for him and held tight. "They've got to be here."

"We should leave before the bogle finds us," Julian warned. "We are not safe here. This is its domain." He gently took the rag-covered diamond from her hand.

Brandi gasped as bright, white illumination shot forth from the stone, lighting the void ahead of them. Julian wriggled his fingers in the air and the golden glow of his protective magic infused them both. Not that it did much good. The light only penetrated so far into the distance. But light, however little, was a welcome presence in the bleakness surrounding them. "This should help keep the bogle at bay until we can get ourselves out of here," he said, handing the diamond back to her.

"Nick," she called out again, desperate. "Where are you?"

There came a noise ahead of them and Brandi ran toward it, ignoring Julian's attempts to keep her at his side. Giving up on coaxing her back, he ran alongside her and added his shouts to her own, grabbing her hand and holding it as they flew together toward the sound.

There came the faint, tinkling sound of a child's voice.

Her heart nearly stopped and even Julian's silence screamed his incredulity.

"Aunt Brandi," they heard through the void.

"I'll be dammed," Julian said in awe. "It cannot be. Can it? It's him. Isn't it?"

"Nick baby, where are you?" Brandi cried out once more, peering into the gloom.

"I'm here," came his faint reply. "I hear you. But I can't see."

She followed his voice. "Keep talking, pumpkin. I'm coming."

He yelled for her over and over again.

Finding some hidden reserve of strength, Brandi ran faster, letting go of Julian's hand. And then, suddenly, her nephew was in her arms.

"Oh baby!" she cried, kissing him all over his face. He was just as she remembered him. His face in the glow of Julian's light was the same sweet face she'd last seen three years ago.

Despite the years, the pain and fear and worry he must have experienced, he hadn't aged a day.

"There are other children here. Do you know where they are?" she asked.

Nodding, his hollow eyes drank her in. "Lost," he said with innocent frankness. "They're lost."

Brandi clutched him tight to her. "Are they still here, are they still alive?"

Nick shook his head and sank deep into her embrace as only a child could have done. "They're all gone. I'm the only one left," he said. "I wanted to leave with them. But…I kept thinking of you. I knew you were looking for me. I kept wishing you'd find me and take me back home." He sobbed weakly. "Where's Mama?"

Brandi kissed him fiercely on the cheek. "Mama will be with you soon, baby doll."

"Promise?"

"I promise," she vowed, holding him tighter.

Julian's strong hand settled into the dip of her back, lending her his strength. "He has your Templar blood in him. You called to that part of him for three years and held him here, kept him here, safe from the bogle's appetites." The awe was clear in his tone. "I never thought such a thing would be possible, but you did it."

"We have to get out of here," she said, cradling her nephew against her, determined that nothing, not even death, would tear them apart now.

"Come with me," Julian said. "I'm not sure where we'll come out, but I feel our way lies in this direction." He grabbed her arm and led her in the darkness.

They ran until they were both breathless. Time passed. And finally, at last, there was a faint light apart from Julian's waiting at the end of the void.

Brandi was the first one through. She fell forward onto the cold floor, rolling so that Nick was protected from their fall. Bright, white light filled her vision. Then Julian was with them.

They had fallen out of the mop closet in the grocery store in town. Julian helped Brandi up. There came the sound of a dozen people gasping and Brandi knew they were in deep shit.

"B-Brandi?" Melissa Holmes, the cashier, said.

The store erupted into chaos. Nick burrowed deeper into Brandi's arms, frightened by all the noise and hubbub around him. She soothed him, kissing his soft hair and eying the customers surrounding them. "I have to get home," she told them. She turned to Julian. "I have to get Nick out of here."

Julian nodded and led a path through the crowd. In seconds they were outside in the bright, warm sunshine.

"How long were we gone?" she asked Julian.

"Hours," he said. "It's afternoon already."

Nick stirred in her arms.

"Is he too heavy?" Julian asked.

"No, he's perfect," Brandi said, tears in her voice.

"Give him to me, Brandi."

"No." She pulled away from Julian's outstretched hands.

"I need to tamper with his memory."

"What do you mean, tamper?" she asked defensively. "Will it hurt him?"

"I can make him forget his fear and pain, those three years in the void. I must—the memories could eventually drive him mad if they aren't dimmed. Let me have him."

Brandi reluctantly handed her nephew over to him and watched as Julian traced familiar designs into the air. Golden light surrounded both him and the child and Julian bent to whisper words into Nick's ear. Nick fell slack against him and Brandi cried out. "Don't worry," Julian reassured her. "He's merely sleeping."

"When he wakes…" She faltered.

"He won't remember everything. And what he remembers will be numbed, distant. He won't suffer much."

"I have to call Gail. I have to let her know he's all right."

"We need to get home first. Away from all these people." It was then that Brandi noticed the small crowd that had gathered around them. She wondered idly if they had seen

Julian's magic and decided it didn't matter. Let them be shocked and amazed, she'd put up with their derision for three years. Julian called Marduk with his cell phone and told him where to pick them up and they began walking down the street, away from the mob.

Sirens wailed in the distance, growing closer. Two police cars, complete with flashing lights, pulled up in front of them. Agent Perez and Agent Thread stepped out of one vehicle and rushed toward them.

"You're under arrest, Ms. Carroll, for kidnapping," Perez said, brandishing a pair of handcuffs.

"She's innocent," Julian protested.

"Then what is a child, missing for three years, doing in your custody?" Thread asked.

"We found him. In the void." Brandi told the truth without hesitating. "But we couldn't find any of the others."

"You have the right to remain silent—"

"You're arresting the wrong person," Julian said.

"And just who are you?" Thread asked angrily.

Julian sighed. "I'm a friend of Ms. Carroll's. And I'm the one you should be arresting. Not Brandi."

Brandi gasped. "No, Julian," she started, but he shushed her. He murmured, too low for the others to hear. "You're more important. Get the diamond back to Ramiel and Marduk. They'll take you the rest of the way. We need to move quickly if we are to save any more innocent lives."

Thread looked at him and shook his head. "I'll just arrest the both of you," he said.

"No," Julian said firmly. "She has no real idea what happened. She's completely innocent. Just listen to her and you'll know I'm right. She's delusional—doesn't want to admit the truth even to herself. I'm the one you want. I'm the one who took the children." Something in Julian's voice resonated and compelled. Brandi knew instinctively, without a doubt, he was using his magic on the agents, forcing them to believe him. "You've my confession, let her go."

Agent Thread and Agent Perez looked at each other, as if silently commiserating on what to do. Brandi cried out as Agent Thread grabbed Julian's hands, cuffed them then escorted him to one of the waiting cruisers. Agent Perez came and took Nick from her, despite her struggles to keep him. He took the still-sleeping child to another cruiser and got into the car with Nick in his arms, leaving Brandi to stand there, alone and dazed on the street as they left.

* * * * *

"We have to get him out," Brandi said without preamble.

Marduk and Ramiel sat at her kitchen table, watching her pace the floor. "How would we do that?" Marduk asked.

"I don't know. Create a diversion or something. Pull a Houdini—don't you watch television? Can't you think of anything?"

"All I can think of is how important it is to do as Julian says and take you straight to Montmartre."

Brandi snorted. "I'm not going anywhere without Julian."

Ramiel and Marduk shared a look. "Brandi, I don't see how we—" Marduk started, before Ramiel interjected.

"I believe I can get him out if you were to create a diversion," he told them, voice tinkling like the chorus of a hundred bells.

"What trick could we pull that would draw everyone's attention away from Julian?" Marduk asked.

Brandi thought for a moment and then inspiration struck. "I might have an idea."

"Of course you might," Marduk sighed.

"No, I think it might work."

"What's your plan?" both Marduk and Ramiel asked in unison.

"Just follow my lead," she told them and raced to her bedroom. In a nightstand drawer there was a pistol, which had belonged to Gail's husband before they'd left the house to Brandi. She made sure it wasn't loaded and shoved it into the waistband of her jeans.

She led Marduk and Ramiel out to her truck and revved the engine high. The vehicle spit gravel as she took off. "Give me your cell phone," she said to Marduk. He handed it to her and she dialed the number for the local police department.

They picked up on the third ring. "Hello, I'd like to report a sighting of those missing children," she said in a nasally voice that she hoped sounded nothing like her own. She gave the dispatcher on the phone directions to the woodlands behind her house and hung up quickly before the woman could ask any further questions.

"Just what are we doing, Brandi?" Marduk asked impatiently.

"We're getting Julian out of jail," she said testily.

"I know that, but how?"

"I figured I'd just play it by ear, you know?" she said with a flippancy she did not feel. "Actually, I'm pretty sure the way will clear itself if we just cooperate with fate."

Ramiel laughed. The sound surprised them all, including Ramiel, who ended his laughter as quickly as he had begun it. If it were possible, his laughter was even more beautiful than his voice. And for the first time since meeting him, Brandi felt her heart soften toward the vampire. Any being who was capable of such beauty couldn't be all bad, she thought.

To fill the sudden silence, Brandi put a cassette into the old truck's tape deck and let the soothing, inspiring sounds of The Cure's *Disintegration* album wash over them. It was a long while before any of them spoke again.

When at last they came to a stop in a parking space in front of the local jail, Brandi looked to Marduk. "Keep the truck running. It won't be long. Ramiel, are you ready?"

"Always."

"Then let's do it."

Brandi got out of the truck and looked around. It was a weekday, late afternoon, and luckily there weren't very many people about. Brandi had counted on this and was glad for the reprieve. She grabbed the gun out of her jeans and nodded toward Ramiel. He seemed to read her thoughts, leading the way into the jail.

There were only three policemen. Brandi gave a heartfelt sigh of relief, grateful that she lived in such a small town. She saw Julian almost immediately, occupying one of the two cells. He looked stunned to see her. Brandi forced herself to look away for fear she might falter in her task.

She waved the gun wildly. "Everybody freeze!" she said with a solid authority she did not feel, and a clichéd dramatis she certainly did.

The police officers obeyed at once.

"Give me the keys to Julian's cell," she demanded.

They did nothing.

Brandi repeated her command. "Give them to me *now*."

Ramiel came between them. "Let me handle this, Brandi—as I assume that's why you wanted me along," he said dryly. Something deep and layered entered his voice. "You will give the keys to Brandi," he told them.

As if they were automatons, the officers all moved at once to do Ramiel's bidding. One of the jailors had the ring of keys on his belt and it took him a few moments to get them free because his colleague was reaching for them at the same time. Finally wrenching the keys free, he threw them to Brandi, never once blinking. Ramiel had them all well under his spell.

With shaking hands, Brandi rushed to the cell where Julian waited, feeling the press of time like a weight on her shoulders.

"I told you to get to Paris," he barked by way of greeting.

"You're welcome," she said, finding the key that unlocked the cell. He was free in seconds and she rushed into his waiting arms. Though it had only been a couple of hours, it had felt as if a lifetime had separated them. "God, I almost lost it," she told him. "Don't ever do something like this again, I couldn't bear it."

Julian kissed her on the forehead and took her hand. "I assume you have transport?"

"Yeah, out front. We need to hurry. They might have Hartsfield airport watched if we wait too long."

"Marduk has a passport for her," Ramiel said softly. "We can leave immediately."

"Great. We'll get on the first flight out of Atlanta," he said, leading them out of the jail, ignoring the vacant stares of the three police officers as they passed.

Ramiel jumped into the bed of the truck, leaving Julian and Brandi to climb into the cab with Marduk. Brandi saw a group of people outside the jailhouse and she leaned out the window. "This is what you get for not believing me!" she shouted, giving them the finger.

Julian hauled her back into the cab. "Why did you do something so foolish?" he asked, his words were angry but the tight hold he kept on her belied his disappointment. "You should have gone on without me. I would have been fine."

"I can't do this without you, Julian," she said. "I just can't."

Julian smiled and kissed her temple. "You're a stubborn piece of baggage, aren't you, love?"

Brandi returned his smile, saying nothing, settling back in the safe cage of his arms.

Thanks to Marduk's speedy driving, they made it to the Atlanta airport in less than an hour.

Chapter Eighteen

After a tense check through customs, they were on their way to Paris. Gregori had met them at Hartsfield with the remaining five keys. The spear of destiny; an ancient ring that Julian told her had once belonged to King Solomon; a piece of the True Cross; the finger bone of Saint Drogo, patron saint of shepherds; and a piece of Mary Magdalene's funeral veil were all accounted for. They climbed aboard their flight with the briefcase of artifacts in hand, Julian having somehow secreted the contents through security.

It was night now and most of the first-class passengers were sleeping, but Brandi, Julian, Ramiel and Marduk were all wide awake. Brandi and Julian sat in the middle third row and Marduk and Ramiel sat directly behind them. They were each planning their next move.

"How will this work?" she asked Julian for what must have been the tenth time.

"I told you, I'm not absolutely certain. But I feel sure that I'll know once we get there. Fate has yet to lead us astray. I've been playing this thing by ear for three decades and I'll trust in my luck to get us past any problems that might arise."

Brandi clutched his hand tight. "I'm a little scared," she confessed. "Okay, I'm really scared."

Julian brought her hand to his mouth and kissed her knuckles. "You? Afraid? Aren't you the one who's been hunting a malevolent spirit for the past three years? You aren't scared. Nothing can unsettle you." He grinned.

Brandi shook her head. "I don't know what to expect. Of course I'm scared."

"A little apprehension is expected. But don't worry," he rushed to console her. "We'll be all right."

Behind them, Ramiel and Marduk were having their own conversation.

"I have no wish to be banished to the void," Ramiel said.

"You won't be," Marduk reassured him. "And neither will I. We're not evil, you and me. We're just...otherworldly."

"I have done much evil in my past," Ramiel pointed out.

"Your idea of evil and my idea of evil differ greatly, my friend."

"I have killed," Ramiel spat, his face a contradicting portrait of rage and regret.

"But you killed those who richly deserved it. Thieves, rapists, murderers. I know you better than you realize, Ramiel, and I tell you once more that when the gate opens you will have nothing to fear."

Ignoring the softly spoken words behind them, Brandi leaned in close to Julian. "Kiss me," she whispered.

Julian took her face in his hands and kissed her, letting his tongue trace over her lips erotically. The kiss lasted several long heartbeats then Julian broke off, breathing raggedly. "I want you," he said.

"I want you too," she said. "Maybe there's room in the bathroom. I always wanted to join the mile-high club."

Julian laughed. "Why don't we make love right here instead?"

Brandi blushed, shocked. "Are you crazy? Anyone could see."

"What Templar is worth his salt who cannot spin an illusion? I can make it so that no one sees. They'll notice nothing out of the ordinary, I assure you."

"But what about Marduk and Ramiel?"

"They won't see, I promise."

"Oh my god!" she gasped. "I can't believe I'm actually entertaining this notion."

"Just trust me," he said, reaching for her.

It felt wicked and dangerous and Brandi's pulse beat a ragged tattoo. Julian pulled her across the seat and settled her on his lap with her back to his chest. His hands rose and cupped her breasts, kneading them until she was breathless. Brandi looked around guiltily and saw that, indeed, no one was paying them any attention. It still didn't lessen the feeling of danger. Brandi could see people all around them, so naturally she felt they could see her too. It was a most wicked feeling.

Brandi had changed earlier into a soft wool skirt and light cotton sweater she had bought at one of the airports they had trudged through. Julian's hands slid beneath her skirt easily, stroking her inner thighs with expert ease. He hooked his hand in the ribbons on her thong panties and pulled them down. He cupped the globes of her bottom in his hands, cherishing her tender flesh. His hands then sought out the wet heat of her welcoming pussy.

He lifted and separated the moist, pink folds, searching out her clitoris with his questing fingertips. "You're already soaking wet for me, baby, and I've barely touched you," he said with such satisfaction in his voice that Brandi blushed once more to the roots of her hair.

Julian's hands moved back, working on the fastening of his trousers. Brandi felt the large, heavy weight of his cock spring free at her back. He lifted her skirts higher, exposing her to any eyes that wished to see, though none of the passengers so much as glanced their way. He rubbed his cock against the cleft of her buttocks, teasing her. Tormenting her. Brandi moaned, biting the sound off at once for fear of alerting anyone.

No one so much as stirred.

"Be as loud as you want, love. No one will hear you," he reassured her, putting his hands beneath her sweater, peeling back her front-clasping bra before at last zeroing in on her aching, swollen nipples. Brandi felt her head fall back, exposing the long line of her throat.

Julian's lips found the shell of her ear and nibbled her there before moving down to nuzzle the side of her neck. Brandi giggled then sighed as he gave her a lover's mark. She looked around, still nervous that someone might notice, but again, no one seemed to see them. Brandi decided to give herself over to the moment. Being out in the open, yet safe from prying eyes, had a dangerously erotic quality to it that had her pulse pounding and her juices flowing.

Grasping his thick erection in his hand, he urged her to lean forward. His fingers found her opening, and he guided the head of his cock into her from behind. He slid in easily, stretching her deliciously, her body quaking around his. His hands grasped her hips and pulled her down hard onto him. Brandi let out a whoosh of air and nearly came as he slid balls-deep into her soaking wet heat.

Julian eased her back and bit her neck delicately, leaving another mark behind, and rocked her on top of him. They moved slowly at first, completely silent, each lost in the wonder of being joined together again. Then Brandi felt her body tighten and knew she wasn't far from climaxing. She began a rougher, faster ride, feeling him slide in and out like a piston impaling her body over and over again. Julian groaned at her back and the sound sent Brandi flying.

At the height of her climax, Julian slipped one finger into her anus and she screamed, her release intensifying exponentially.

A second later, Julian's body pulsed inside hers and jettisoned his cum deep within her body.

Several long moments later, Julian pulled her free of his impalement and sat her back in her seat beside him. He dropped to his knees and knelt before her, spreading her legs wide with his hands. His head darted between her legs, finding her wet pussy glistening, swollen and ready for his kiss. He licked a long line from her anus to her clit and Brandi felt tears spring forth from the corner of her eyes as he drove her body to new heights.

He kissed her, using his whole face to caress and titillate. He licked and nibbled, kissed and suckled. And when he found her clit, he sucked it like he would have sucked her nipples, using his lips, teeth and tongue to drive her wild. He slid two fingers into her, hooking them up and rubbing deliciously over her G-spot. Her body shuddered and she moaned helplessly, thrashing her head against the seat.

A long, low groan escaped her lips as she came once more. Julian's tongue went wild on her then, exploring every fold, every slick inch of her. He moaned against her, vibrating her most tender flesh so that she came all the harder. Brandi saw spots dance before her eyes and knew she was close to passing out.

The last of her tremors subsided and she lay limp and useless in her seat. Julian quickly righted her clothing and then righted his own. He sat down next to her once more and took her under his arm. "Calm down now, love. Rest. You'll need your energy for the hours ahead."

Body replete and relaxed as it had never been before, Brandi slept and, for the first time in three years, her dreams did not become nightmares.

* * * * *

Montmartre, a small village overlooking the sprawling city of Paris, France, was full of tourists despite the fact that it was a regular weekday. Artists with large notebooks of drawing paper peddled their talents to any willing to pay for a portrait of their time spent in the famous hamlet, and dozens of shops sold original paintings courtesy of the local artisans. Art and inspiration were a living, breathing thing here, a palpable presence in the air that none could ignore.

Brandi and Julian, hands clasped tightly together, trudged up the steep hill that led to the Sacré-Coeur basilica. Ramiel and Marduk followed at a safe distance behind them, stern countenances warning off the beggars and street performers who would have crossed their paths otherwise. The weather was crisp and cool, and a soft breeze continually stirred the air as they ascended higher and higher.

The basilica was breathtaking and enormous. Its rounded white towers stretched high into the sky, reaching toward the heavens. It was full and round, almost feminine in shape. The stones were so white that Brandi had to squint her eyes against the bright glare of the church in the afternoon sunlight.

"Where is the gate?" Brandi asked.

"Well, it's not exactly a physical gate."

"What do you mean?" she asked.

"You'll see what I mean when we get there," Julian told her. He led them to the steps of the church, but instead of going in, he swerved and led them to the side of the massive structure. Steep stairs led downward, into the cold and unforgiving stone of the underground catacombs that rested beneath Sacré-Coeur, and Julian tugged gently on Brandi's hand to take her down the pathway.

They disappeared into the darkness of the catacombs. There were people here as well, tourists come to see the ancient tombs within, but Julian and the others paid them little heed. They came to an open doorway, dark and smelling of cold, wet mold.

"Through there," Julian said, still holding tight to Brandi's hand.

Brandi followed him through, deeper into the forbidding darkness. A hundred feet from the entrance, old bones and burial boxes littered crevices carved into the stone walls. The sounds of the tourists had long faded behind them, and the light that came from the entranceway dimmed into nothingness. Julian made a few gestures with his hands and light flared to life, surrounding them in a warm, golden glow that fought off the oppressive darkness. Brandi breathed a huge sigh of relief, not even having realized how frightened she had grown in the gathering dark.

After several long minutes of walking farther into the crypt, Brandi and her group came upon an outcropping of rock in the wall. It looked out of place, as if it had just recently sprung out of the ground. A crude circle of stones surrounded it. If Brandi hadn't been looking so hard she would have missed them, but it was clear, after careful study, that the stones had been placed there by intelligent design.

"It's there," Julian pointed.

Brandi could only see the giant rock. "But there's no door."

"Not yet," he told her. "But there will be. Marduk, put the keys on those six rocks there."

Marduk moved to the circle of stones and decided how best to position the keys. Julian gave Brandi a quick squeeze and told her to stand in the center of the stones, directly in front of the large outcropping of rock.

"Now what?" Brandi asked.

Julian ignored her, instead closing his eyes and muttering something under his breath as his fingers made little designs in the air. An electric charge sparked in the air, surrounded them with energy—even Marduk and Ramiel—and Brandi knew instinctively that this was a protection charm meant to keep them all as safe as possible.

Marduk placed the keys, one apiece, on the waiting stones. He was careful, respectful, even Brandi could see the reverence with which he moved. It was clear that he knew this was a holy and magical place. Brandi could feel the air charged by both Julian's magic and the magic of the very ground they trod upon.

Marduk placed the last of the keys upon its resting place. The air seemed to still and Brandi's ears popped. She felt something tremble inside her and realized it was caused by the ground shaking beneath her feet. It moved slightly at first, easily mistaken for imagination, but then the movements grew more and more pronounced, nearly tripping Brandi where she stood. The earth moved with a mighty groan and dust flew about them, blinding Brandi, cutting her adrift in the storm of sand and debris that swirled around her. She heard Julian call out something, but she couldn't hear what it was. And it didn't matter…something was taking hold of her.

She looked at the wall of stone before her and felt a buzzing sensation in the back of her head. Without meaning to, she reached out and placed one of her hands on the rock. The earth heaved again beneath her feet, but she stood firm, keeping her hand on the rock in front of her. She was held transfixed. Without knowing what she needed to do next, she focused her will on that one hand that lay against the cold, wet stone.

With a start, Brandi realized that she could *feel* the presence of the other stones. They called to her, as if they were singing her name over and over again in an ancient language only she could understand. Something cold and malevolent wrapped itself around her heart and she cried out, feeling a lancing pain in her chest. She called for Julian but heard no answer in the rising din.

Blackness. Sudden and absolute. Rays of an even deeper darkness shot out on either side of her, opening a great, gaping maw that surrounded her and bled beyond. Her hand, still on the stone, was the only thing real to her in that moment. All else was madness.

The cries of a thousand lost souls bombarded her ears and she cried out once more. She tried to pull her hand away, but it stayed glued to the rock, effectively trapping her within the swelling storm of darkness.

"Push it back," she heard Julian shout above the cacophony.

And then she knew what to do. It was as if a switch had flipped in her mind, lighting her way. She pushed at the darkness with her will, shoving her hand hard against the stone for emphasis. The streamers of darkness seemed to freeze in the air, then, with a loud explosion of sand-filled air, the darkness turned inward on itself.

A hurricane would seem like a whisper to the roaring sound that now engulfed her. Her ears and head rang with the cries and screams of black, evil things that were now being sucked past her and into the black hole she had somehow opened. Hundreds, *thousands* of beings swept past her, so fast she couldn't see, but rather felt them as they passed. The wind roared, thick and cold and vile. It stank of evil, making Brandi gag uncontrollably, and she sank helplessly to her knees, hand still held frozen to the rock.

Brandi heard Ramiel yell one second before he flew by. She reached out immediately and grabbed his hand, holding on for dear life. She saw the red glow of his eyes and for once they did not frighten her. As if a curtain had opened before her, she read his soul and knew that no matter what, she mustn't let him go into the void. He was a vampire, a creature of darkness, but he was not evil. He was completely alone, cut adrift from his own kind and from mankind. Yet he still fought for the good of man. He gave himself selflessly, honor bound to a cause that did not even allow for those of his ilk to exist.

"Don't let go!" he called to her, face even paler than usual, panic clear in his eyes. "Brandi—"

"I won't," she vowed. "I won't let you go, I promise! And don't you let go, either, Fang Face."

Ramiel laughed, but the joyous sound was short-lived. He gasped. "I'm slipping," he said, glancing back with trepidation at the darkness that threatened to swallow him whole.

"No you're not," she said firmly, tightening her grip. "Ramiel, I know you're not evil. You're just dark and there's nothing wrong with that, not when you strive so hard to be light. You're not going into that void, okay? I won't let you."

Ramiel grunted and held tight as the maelstrom hurled around them.

With one hand glued to the rock in front of her and one hand holding tight to Ramiel, Brandi felt as if she might be torn apart. But she was determined not to let go of the vampire. She knew they had their differences. He was a predator after all and she was just a human. But she knew, deep in her heart, that Ramiel was more than his scary exterior. She vowed to herself that she would not let him go, if only for Julian's sake. She knew he, most of all, would regret the loss of his friend.

Brandi felt that strange tickle in the back of her mind once more and knew it was time to close the rift that she had opened. She focused, imagining the blackness fading away to nothingness.

Nothing happened.

She focused harder, *needing* to close the rift.

Ramiel began to slip from her fingers.

"Don't you dare!" she yelled and strengthened her grip. "I'm not letting you go!"

With a great push of her will, the horrible cacophony quieted. Imperceptibly, but nonetheless it began to die down. There weren't so many forms and shapes flying by her now and Brandi hoped she had left the door open long enough. Regardless, she couldn't stand for the void to be opened any longer. She pushed again and felt the other six keys working with her to shut the gate. Their power flowed through her like lava, warming her where the darkness had chilled her. She felt their magical strength swell.

The black doorway shrank, growing smaller and smaller. A great explosion shook the ground—and the way was shut with a deafening boom.

Ramiel dropped to the ground and Brandi at last was able to claim her hand back from the rock wall. She felt her breath sob in and out of her lungs and waited for her eyes to adjust to the sudden brightness of Julian's magic as it swelled around them once more.

"My god. My god. I thank you, Brandi," Ramiel said, as breathless as she, red eyes fading to black once more. "I owe you everything."

"No problem," she said with a lightheartedness she didn't feel. She was exhausted, wrung out and completely beside herself with lingering fright.

Julian rushed to take her up in his arms. "Are you all right, love?" Brandi nodded and buried her face in the crook of his neck. "It's over now," he cooed to her gently. "It's over."

Marduk helped Ramiel to his feet. "I thought I had lost you there for a moment," he said.

A flash of fang proved that he was doing better than Brandi, as he shook his friend's hand heartily, smiling. "I thought so too, but thanks to Brandi, I am no longer in any danger."

"Come on, let's get the— Where are the keys?" Julian exclaimed.

Marduk and Ramiel looked about them at the stones on the ground, where the six keys of Solomon had once sat. They were gone, as if they had never been.

"Where did they go?" Brandi asked, voice hoarse.

"Displacement," Marduk said. "They've been flung to the corners of the world. We'll have to start searching for them all over again."

"We'll find them again. Don't worry," Julian told him. "We needn't feel so pressured in this new search. We've already opened the gate and banished evil. We won't have such a great need for them again for many decades."

"What about the Hope? I had thought to return it to its rightful place in the Smithsonian once we had finished our quest," Marduk said.

"I suppose the fake one will have to remain where it is for a while longer," Ramiel said softly.

Julian chuckled. "I wonder when the discrepancy will be noticed."

"Come on," Marduk said impatiently. "Let's get back to the hotel. I need rest…and I never need rest! I can only imagine how exhausted Brandi must feel."

Brandi didn't answer for she was already asleep in Julian's arms.

Epilogue

ಐ

"I can't go back home," Brandi said with a sigh. "I'm a wanted criminal now." She snuggled deeper into the covers of the bed, hiding her nudity.

Julian pulled the covers from her, exposing her once more and gathering her close to him. "Don't worry about it. All it will take is some memory tampering. Granted, that will take some time, but if you'd like you can return to your home."

"Where else would I go?" she asked.

"Where I go," Julian said softly.

Brandi caught her breath. "You mean stay with you?"

"Yes."

"For how long? I'm warning you, you'll get bored with me eventually. I'm not all that exciting, you know," she told him with no small amount of trepidation. "Without the drama of the past few years I'll just be plain and dull."

Julian was silent for a time. "Let me get something from my suitcase." He leaned over and kissed her. "I'll be right back."

He was gone for only a few minutes, coming back with a velvet bag that held something large within it. He sat on the foot of the bed and opened the bag, revealing a strange, misshapen cup.

"What is that?" she asked, frowning. It was quite ugly. Crude even.

"This is the Holy Grail," he told her with a smile.

Brandi felt her eyes bulge. *"What?"*

"The Holy Grail. The cup of life. I brought it with the hope that you might drink from it."

"What are you saying?" she asked breathlessly.

"I want you at my side always, Brandi. You're mine now. We could spend eternity together. I *want* us to spend eternity together. As I have never wanted anything before."

Brandi felt her heart sink into despair. "I can't. I-I want more." She took a deep breath. "You don't love me," she said. "You can't love me. You barely know me."

Julian smiled tenderly. "You're the most stubborn woman I've ever met. You've a sense of honesty about you that very, very few people possess. And you have courage in spades. You've proven yourself a hundred times."

"But all that doesn't matter."

"Of course it matters. Baby, you have saved the world today. You're a true hero. How could I not love you?"

"Y-you love me?" She felt tears sting her eyes. "You do? No one but my family has ever loved me before."

"And I will love you forever," he vowed. "Will you drink from this cup and join me in eternal life?"

Eternal life. Could such a thing be possible? She was so happy. She couldn't begin to imagine a life full of such happiness, not after the nightmare she had lived for the past three years. But she wanted that happiness, that joy. The joy of being in love forever.

"We'll fight. I'm not easy to get along with, even I'll admit to that," she warned him.

"Neither am I. We're a good match, don't you think?"

Brandi laughed. "Are you sure you want to do this?"

Julian took her face in his hands and kissed her tenderly on the lips. "I'm sure," he said, pulling back.

"What if you change your mind?"

"I could never change my mind. I've never felt this way about another woman—not in all my years. You're the one for me. And I know I'm the one for you, if you'll just admit it."

"Oh Julian, this is too much."

"Do you love me?" he asked.

Brandi searched her heart, imagined a life without Julian and knew her answer. "I do." Her answer was absolute. "I do love you, Julian."

"Then drink from this cup and wed your soul to mine," he said with a smile.

"Okay," she said. "But first..." She pulled him to her. "Make love to me."

With a rakish smile, Julian flipped her over on the bed. He took her from behind, slamming home with one mighty thrust. The wet, sucking sounds of their bodies filled the air around them as he began to slowly ride her. Brandi's breasts bobbed with each thrust and Julian's hands came around her to hold them steady. His fingers toyed with her nipples, tugging and squeezing them delicately.

Passion consumed them, flinging them higher and higher into the heavens. Julian came first, pulling himself free of her body at the last minute and spending himself on the entrance of her anus. He slipped and slid through their combined juices and, still semi-hard, he began to slide the head of his penis into her ass.

"You're so fucking tight," he groaned.

One of his hands reached around her and found her clit, rubbing it in little circles with the tips of his fingers. Brandi cried out and moved back against him, sending his cock even deeper into her ass. She cried out again, shuddering, body stretched tight on a rack of pleasure-pain. "Oh god, yes, yes, *yes*," she panted. "Oh please, take me, *take me*." She was babbling, she knew, but she couldn't stop.

He rubbed her clit and sent her soaring. Her body tightened, her anus clenching his cock tight. Julian groaned long and loud and came once more, deep inside her, burning her with each spurt of his cum.

"I love you, Brandi. I truly do," he panted, collapsing on top of her.

Brandi didn't mind the weight at all, but was happy when he moved next to her, turning her to face him. "I love you too," she vowed, knowing it to be the truest thing she'd ever said.

They kissed, sharing their lips, teeth and tongues. The kiss lasted for what felt like hours and they fell into a light doze, their mouths and hearts joined.

The Grail fell off the bed, unheeded, to the floor. It pulsed with a cheerful, golden light then faded back into obscurity.

Also by Sherri L. King

eBooks:

Bachelorette
Beyond Illusion
Ellora's Cavemen: Tales from the Temple III (*anthology*)
Ferocious
Fetish
Full Moon Xmas
Hung Like a Dead Man
Horde Wars: Ravenous
Horde Wars: Wanton Fire
Horde Wars: Razor's Edge
Horde Wars: Lord of the Deep
Lover's Key
Midnight Desires (*anthology*)
Moon Lust
Moon Lust: Bitten
Moon Lust: Feral Heat
Moon Lust: Mating Season
Rayven's Awakening
Sacred Eden
Sanctuary
Sexy Beast
Shikar: Caress of Flame
Shikar: Ride the Lightning

Sin and Salvation
Sterling Files 1: Steele
Sterling Files 2: Vicious
Sterling Files 3: Fyre
Sterling Files 4: Hyde
Sterling Files: Selfless
The Jewel
Venereus

Print Books:
Bedtime, Playtime
Bitten
Caress of Flame
Ellora's Cavemen: Tales from the Temple III (*anthology*)
Fetish
Fever-Hot Dreams
Forbidden Fantasies
His Fantasies, Her Dreams
Hyde
Insatiable (Pocket)
Lord of the Deep
Manaconda (*anthology*)
Primal Heat
Ravenous
Razor's Edge
Rayven's Awakening
Ride the Lightning
Sterling Files
Wanton Fire
White Hot Holidays Volume 2 (*anthology*)

About the Author

෨

Sherri King lives in the American Midwest with her husband, artist and illustrator Darrell King. Hailed by industry officials as an e-pub phenomenon, Sherri is the author of critically acclaimed series The Horde Wars and Sterling Files, as well as the horror lit-erotica, *Venereus*. She is currently at work on *Traveler's Kiss*, book six in The Horde Wars, due out in 2010 with Ellora's Cave Publishing.

Sherri welcomes comments from readers. You can find her website and email address on her author bio page at www.ellorascave.com.

Tell Us What You Think

We appreciate hearing reader opinions about our books. You can email us at Comments@EllorasCave.com.

Why an electronic book?

We live in the Information Age—an exciting time in the history of human civilization, in which technology rules supreme and continues to progress in leaps and bounds every minute of every day. For a multitude of reasons, more and more avid literary fans are opting to purchase e-books instead of paper books. The question from those not yet initiated into the world of electronic reading is simply: *Why?*

1. *Price.* An electronic title at Ellora's Cave Publishing and Cerridwen Press runs anywhere from 40% to 75% less than the cover price of the exact same title in paperback format. Why? Basic mathematics and cost. It is less expensive to publish an e-book (no paper and printing, no warehousing and shipping) than it is to publish a paperback, so the savings are passed along to the consumer.

2. *Space.* Running out of room in your house for your books? That is one worry you will never have with electronic books. For a low one-time cost, you can purchase a handheld device specifically designed for e-reading. Many e-readers have large, convenient screens for viewing. Better yet, hundreds of titles can be stored within your new library—on a single microchip. There are a variety of e-readers from different manufacturers. You can also read e-books on your PC or laptop computer. (Please note that Ellora's Cave does not endorse any specific brands.

You can check our websites at www.ellorascave.com or www.cerridwenpress.com for information we make available to new consumers.)
3. *Mobility.* Because your new e-library consists of only a microchip within a small, easily transportable e-reader, your entire cache of books can be taken with you wherever you go.
4. *Personal Viewing Preferences.* Are the words you are currently reading too small? Too large? Too... ANNOYING? Paperback books cannot be modified according to personal preferences, but e-books can.
5. *Instant Gratification.* Is it the middle of the night and all the bookstores near you are closed? Are you tired of waiting days, sometimes weeks, for bookstores to ship the novels you bought? Ellora's Cave Publishing sells instantaneous downloads twenty-four hours a day, seven days a week, every day of the year. Our webstore is never closed. Our e-book delivery system is 100% automated, meaning your order is filled as soon as you pay for it.

Those are a few of the top reasons why electronic books are replacing paperbacks for many avid readers.

As always, Ellora's Cave and Cerridwen Press welcome your questions and comments. We invite you to email us at Comments@ellorascave.com or write to us directly at Ellora's Cave Publishing Inc., 1056 Home Avenue, Akron, OH 44310-3502.

Discover for yourself why readers can't get enough of the multiple award-winning publisher
Ellora's Cave.
Whether you prefer e-books or paperbacks,
be sure to visit EC on the web at
www.ellorascave.com
for an erotic reading experience that will leave you breathless.

CPSIA information can be obtained at www.ICGtesting.com
Printed in the USA
LVOW041115060512

280541LV00001B/163/P